T0146732

Some designs are timeless . . .

They grew up together yet worlds apart. But a wealthy young man and a classy young woman find that some bonds can't be broken . . .

The only thing Marigold Reynolds and billionaire Hagen Allbrook ever had in common was their attraction. Marigold made sure that never went anywhere by cutting ties with him six years ago. Now, however, she needs a job—and Hagen's design assistant desperately needs someone to fill in for her at his family's construction firm. Trusting that time has dimmed the electricity between them, Marigold accepts. But as she undertakes his challenging renovation of her own ancestors' home, it's soon clear she's mistaken.

A year after his wife's death, Hagen is coming to terms with the past. He's as drawn to Marigold as ever, but as they finally cross long-held boundaries, a misunderstanding, and Marigold's belief that she can never measure up to his perfect wife, threatens to tear them apart once more. Hagen's only chance of winning her back is to reveal the truth about his marriage. And perhaps then Marigold will reveal a heartfelt secret of her own . . .

Visit us at www.kensingtonbooks.com

Books by Virginia Taylor

South Landers
Starling
Ella
Charlotte
Wenna

Romance By Design
Sets Appeal
Perfect Scents

Golden Opportunity

A Romance By Design Novel

Virginia Taylor

LYRICAL PRESS
Kensington Publishing Corp.
www.kensingtonbooks.com

To RJT – all my love forever.

Chapter 1

In the glimmer of early morning light provided by a high bank of windows, Marigold Reynolds picked her way through white-sheeted furniture, a collection of floor lamps with oddly angled shades, a table needing another leg, and a stack of badly folded canvas sheeting. Two long shelves along the back wall of the warehouse sat blatantly empty while boxes of who-knew-what had been scattered higgledy-piggledy across the long expanse of the concrete floor. Wan picture frames had been huddled together, waiting to fall onto the unwary. For a woman with an orderly mind, this was her idea of being dragged through hell.

The loading bay door she had slid shut after her entry began to rumble open again, and a larger patch of light hovered around the ghostly shapes. She sneezed.

"Is that you, Marigold?"

"I'm over in the far aisle," she called.

The top of Antigone Allbrook's blond head bobbed up behind one of the stacks. Tiggy, a tallish, long-limbed sweetheart, dodged and twisted through the unmarked aisles toward Marigold. "Sorry I'm late." Tiggy was always late.

Marigold was usually early. "I've been exploring." She gave her friend a hug. "I need to know what you've got here if I'm expected to look after it."

"This is pretty well everything." Tiggy glanced around, scratching at her eyebrow. "Though, I often find weird little surprises that I'm sure I haven't seen before. Treasures all," she said in an offhand tone. Her unicorn-pink hair matched her tight jeans, contrasting with her green sneakers and her flowing yellow top. Tiggy had decided long ago that as the artist of the family, she should dress accordingly. "And I won't miss a single one of them."

Marigold laughed. She and Tiggy had met at school, or maybe she had met Calli, her sister, first. The two were identical twins, though Tiggy made sure everyone knew she was the elder. Somehow Marigold and Tiggy had clicked, perhaps because their opposing natures complemented each other. Artistic Tiggy had a wayward streak while unimaginative Marigold was embarrassingly methodical.

Marigold's tidiness hadn't diminished over the years, and Tiggy still hadn't settled down. She had decided to take a break from her job with her father, a property developer, and do something in Cambodia. When Marigold had asked what, Tiggy had shrugged. "Teach orphans to paint?"

From that, Marigold had deduced Tiggy planned to do charity work. She also planned to be back in three months, and she had asked Marigold to take over as AA & Co.'s property developer and event coordinator, the first of a more comprehensive decorating job than Marigold had handled before. "Let's hope I learn where everything is before I break my neck."

"It won't take you any time. You've seen half the props before because you made all the curtains and the cushion covers, and I don't know what-all else."

Marigold had done odd sewing jobs from home for the past six years, and her weekly orders from Tiggy were not only her way of supporting herself but also the highlights in her soulless existence. When everything in her life had consisted of routine trips to the hospital, counting out tablets, cooking special meals, and keeping her mother interested in life, having another focus kept her going. Plus, she needed a steady income. "I hope you have enough here to cover every event."

"Don't worry about that now. Hagen's going to show you around." Tiggy planted her hands on her hips, an expectant smile on her face.

Marigold dragged in a breath and eked it out, her cheeks tingling. She doubted Tiggy's brother Hagen, the golden boy, would be particularly thrilled to see her. He had always been polite, but golden boys were best left to golden girls, not those with a slight tarnish. At school, Marigold's tarnish came from being a poor scholarship student. In those days, Hagen preferred the people who had as much cash to splash around as he did. "It will be very nice to see him again," she said, using her impartial voice.

Tiggy made a wry face. "He's not the same man. Mercia's death knocked the stuffing out of him."

Last year, Hagen's beautiful wife, Mercia, had been killed in a car accident, and at the time Marigold had commiserated with Tiggy. Marigold didn't want to be mean-spirited about the death of anyone, but Hagen's stuffing had been so tight in recent years that he could barely acknowledge her. A little less stuffing might not be so bad. "You left a list of this week's jobs?"

Tiggy found a pocket in her loose cashmere top. "It's a bit messy, but I think you'll understand it."

Marigold skimmed over the words in the torn-out page of a small notebook. She had been dealing with Tiggy's lists for three years now and her writing no longer confounded Marigold. Nor did Tiggy's shorthand. "My biggest problem will be finding things. Where did you leave the furniture for today's staging job?"

"Close to the loading door. It's easiest if you go with the props. I give myself a day for each job when I'm staging a house. I plan a month ahead, if possible, but sometimes I only have days. The events take much longer. The bigger event, the trickier. We often need to hire chairs, but we have most things in the warehouse. I'll wait until Hagen arrives, and then I'll go. My plane leaves this afternoon, and I want to see Calli and Ma before then. Last minute requests in my will." Tiggy laughed.

"Don't even joke about dying, Tiggy." Marigold grabbed Tiggy and hugged her again. "Because if you leave me with this mess for more than three months, I'll kill you."

Tiggy laughed. "Trust me, I'll be back." She smoothed Marigold's carefully tied back hair in a motherly way. "If you hadn't said you would do this, I probably wouldn't have been able to go. I don't know too many people I would trust to take this on, but you're an experienced stager and you know my style. This time of the year we're busy, but I had to get away. I couldn't stay here any longer, letting my life pass me by."

Friend or not, Tiggy hadn't shared her personal problems, but most women's problems stemmed from a man. Likely, Tiggy's did, too. Marigold's didn't. She couldn't remember the last time she'd had a date, and only one man had ever caused her a problem, other than in family matters where males were the cause of all the ructions.

Tiggy let her go and led the way to the furnishings she had picked out for one of the houses in a new row of ten in the western suburbs. AA wanted a single show home readied for publicity photographs before putting the houses on the market later in the month. "The list will tell you what is meant for each room, but you have wriggle space. If anything looks out of place, move it elsewhere. If it looks really odd, you'll need to come back and pick around for what you want. As you know, in the warehouse I keep tables together, chairs together, and the soft furnishings on the shelves."

As Marigold was trying not to look surprised at Tiggy's gross exaggeration of her placement skills, a car drew up outside. The view from the twelve-foot-high open door showed a bleeding, bloody, red Porsche rumbling to a stop in the staff car park. Marigold didn't have to guess who the driver might be. Even in his last year at school, Hagen had owned a nice Mazda sports model. He had no qualms about flashing his parent's cash. If Marigold still had a family, they would have been horrified.

Unlike Hagen, she came from 'old money' but in her case, the money was so old that it had disintegrated and wafted off into the air after three generations. She was the fifth. Her father had snatched a little back, but her mother was his first wife. His second wife lived in comfort with him and his two sons, while Marigold's mother had accepted his half of her house with her child support.

Then, as she and Tiggy watched, the golden boy strolled into the warehouse. Over the years—Hagen would be almost thirty now—the gold had remained. His white-blond hair had darkened somewhat, but in the light of the doorway he stood surrounded by a halo that he could never have earned. If the fates collaborated with justice, a person as endowed with money, brains, and athletic ability as Hagen should be only minimally attractive. Instead, the man was a tall, wide-shouldered heart stopper.

Her breath sighed out as he hesitated and glanced across the shrouded furniture. He spotted Tiggy and lifted a hand. Then his gaze slowly shifted to Marigold. Her mouth dried.

Nothing in the world would let her visibly react. She'd last seen him at Calli's wedding a year ago, but she hadn't spoken to him on that day. His aloof expression had warned off everyone. She managed a polite, if not vague smile. "Hi."

"Marigold with the marigold hair." He sounded surprised, probably because he had finally connected her name with her appearance, but her hair was a dead giveaway. She had been named after the orange of her hair, the name an embarrassment she had tried to argue her mother into letting her change a long time ago.

"It'll be tricky when I go gray." She shrugged. "No one will ever remember me."

"Your hair is aggressively red enough to defy fading."

Even uttering that line, which was mildly funny, he didn't smile. His thick-lashed eyes didn't glint with slow amusement the way they used to. His words seemed to come from someone else, not from the handsome young man she remembered who had the world at his feet, but from a man who would more likely kick the world in passing. Anyone could see Hagen hadn't yet dealt with his grief.

She was also bereaved, though admittedly she'd had time to come to terms with losing the person she loved most. Her mother had passed away little by little. His wife had died on impact when her car had crashed into a tree. "I'll probably adopt the clown red. I'm the eccentric type."

Tiggy sighed loudly. "Civilities completed, I will now leave you to Hagen. I'm off to pack." She kissed Marigold's cheek, kissed Hagen's cheek, and left two people sharing the same heavy silence.

Hagen let out an audible breath. "It's very good of you to take over at such short notice," he said stiffly. "Calli could have done the job, but she's busy on her own projects, or so she says."

"You're implying she's lying?"

He briefly drew his imperious eyebrows together. "I'm using poor phrasing. Calli says she is busy on her own projects. Does that suit you better?"

Marigold decided to smile rather than answer. She could haggle with him all day, but he was her employer now and she had already shifted the boundaries on a burgeoning boss/drudge conversation. "Tiggy said you would show me around."

"You'll have to find your own way around," he said unhelpfully, pushing his hands into the pockets of his perfectly cut gray trousers. His perfectly cut gray jacket sat perfectly misplaced. A thousand dollars wouldn't buy either item. "I have no idea of Tiggy's filing system. She doesn't have one as far as I can tell."

Marigold paused for the beat of three, again holding her words. "I think she meant the main building—her office, and the amenities, etcetera. I know the warehouse because this is where I deliver my goods, but I've never been in her office, and I don't know where to powder my nose, for example."

He glanced at her nose. "That would be old money's way of saying the bathroom, I expect."

"Old money can also say loo, but I wasn't sure if new money would understand." Her heart dropped. Her mother would have been ashamed to hear her talk that way. Descended from the earliest settlers, Sir Patrick and Lady Grace, her mother would never have dreamed of belittling anyone else who had arrived in the country since. "That was ungracious of me."

"And old money is never ungracious." He turned away, as if shutting out the knowledge of a past memory.

"I wouldn't consider it if I stopped to think, but you have to admit you goaded me," she said with an apologetic lift of her shoulders.

He examined the expression on her face, and appeared to lose concentration. "Through that side door is a corridor," he said, his broad shoulders squaring. He averted his gaze and pointed to where the main building, a modern concrete office block, joined onto the warehouse beneath the rest of the building. "That leads to the amenities and to the staff room. You can make tea or coffee or enjoy whatever sugar-loaded filler is currently available. I'll walk you through and show you where my office is. Tiggy's, now yours, is there, too."

"Right," she said as he led the way.

He walked like a cat, using a smooth, athletic stride. A grieving widower or not, he still had an admirable back view, though his suit jacket hid what used to be a very tight behind. His hair had been well-cut, not shorn or trendy, but expensively styled, and brushed back. Even in the throes of mourning, he presented himself like a billionaire's son.

The corridor had been carpeted with industrial gray and the walls were painted a lighter shade. He showed her the all-white bathroom and the facilities, and she was impressed by the staff room, possibly the only staff room she'd seen in her life, other than that at school. This one had the flow-through gray carpeting and the same walls, but bright, modern paintings hung grouped together on one wall. Immediately, the place looked friendly. Tables and chairs sat around the room and a few comfortable armchairs, but the pièce de résistance was the glass servery.

Apparently, with no charge, an employee could help herself to Greek pastries, short breads, custard slices, or a cheese-and-olive platter. Hagen's Greek mother used to be a compulsive feeder of people and apparently hadn't changed since the days when Marigold was hauled by Tiggy into the lovely big house the Allbrooks filled with their noise. Coming from a single-parent household, Marigold couldn't get enough of people shouting with laughter, or arguing obscure and wonderful points. She was a natural arguer of points herself.

"My—*our*—office is two doors farther along."

"Ah. Good placement."

He stared down at her.

"Two doors away from coffee and shortbread? Who would argue that?"

He gave a sideways glance. "Follow me."

Two doors down, he turned into a mini-foyer presided over by a long desk and a middle-aged, black-haired woman who lifted her head and smiled at Hagen. "Good morning. Who's this? Tiggy's wonderful friend?" She aimed her direct brown eyes at Marigold. Her hair had been scraped up into a bun at the crown of her head and she wore her green-framed glasses halfway down her nose.

Marigold smiled. "I don't know how I came to be wonderful but yes, I'm Tiggy's friend."

"You're wonderful because you're taking over from her at a moment's notice." The woman looked amused.

"Marigold, meet Sandra, my personal assistant. If you have any questions, Sandra is more likely to know the answer than I am." With that, Hagen strolled through the door that featured his name added to the title of Business Manager.

Sandra stood and walked over to the other door, marked Antigone Allbrook. "You'll find your work station in here. Tiggy left her appointment book on the desk and she says you know your way around a computer. Any problems, call out."

Marigold walked into her new office and glanced at the computer, fighting the temptation to run back to her car. She wanted to drive home and stay there, dreaming of her old life where computers only featured for the odd e-mail, the odder address, or occasionally for finding a tradesman.

She glanced at the appointment book, but she already knew she would be staging a house today. That was within her comfort zone. Barely. She managed single-contract staging for land agents, but she used the client's furniture fluffed up a little with touches of her own, her homemade cushion covers, or her borrowed furniture. The rest… She warded off a panic attack by concentrating her gaze on Tiggy's messy desk. Tidying up was a job she could handle. Later.

After a few moments of deep breathing, she edged back past Sandra's desk and made her way to the warehouse again. The double doors had been dragged wide open and two men had started shifting a houseful of furniture into a truck marked AA & Co.

"I'm Marigold, the new stager," she called over the noise of the rumbling trolley. "I'll be coming with you. How long will you take to load?"

"An hour, give or take. I'm Billy Bunter." A middle-aged man with a squashed nose like an ex-boxer and a perfectly round bald patch on the back of his head, stopped and grinned at her.

"You're not!"

"I'm Jeff Bunter, but I'm called Billy," he explained, standing patiently with his hands on his hips. "But call me Jeff if you like."

She smiled. "I like Billy."

"He's Joe." Billy indicated the other man with a head of wild dark curls who also looked as if he would be handy in a fight. He nodded at Marigold and grabbed up an armchair.

The two men worked fast, not like normal furniture movers who were paid for the job. These men worked for the company, like Marigold. She wouldn't waste time on the job either, mainly because she didn't know how much time she would need to do the job Tiggy did. She might take twice as long, for all she knew, never having needed to work to a tight schedule. While the men loaded, she checked inside the boxes she had seen scattered in the far aisle, wondering where to put them. Bad mistake. The boxes were full of items returned from a previous staging that ought to be sorted before being stored in their rightful places on a shelf somewhere. Since at this moment the shelves had no discernable order system, she busied herself looking under dust sheets and trying to remember what she had seen where. She couldn't resist shifting a few chairs that appeared to have been filed under tables, to the chair aisle.

By the time the men got to the smaller props, she began stashing items away in the truck, too. Barely an hour later, she was on her way. The unloading worked in reverse. She took the smaller items off and dropped them in the most appropriate rooms. As soon as the curtain rods had been carried into the house, she matched the sizes to the windows, grabbed the ladder, and looked around for the tool kit.

"I can put up the curtain rods if I can borrow a powered screwdriver," she said to Billy, who had dropped a disassembled king-size bed into the largest bedroom.

"I'll get them up for you. You could put that bed together."

"Okay." She sat on the floor with an Allen key and the pieces, but she hadn't assembled a bed before. After a bit of mumbling to herself, she decided which ends fitted with which sides. Then she worked on the slats. Without another job until a mattress arrived, she put together a double bed in each of the two smaller rooms. By this time, the soft furnishings had arrived, and she made up the three beds.

The next two hours flew by. She wondered what Tiggy usually did about lunch, or a drink. Apparently, AA & Co. supplied the food needed during the job. Joe dumped a cardboard box in the kitchen and pulled out individual meal packs of salads, sandwiches, and fruit. He also took out an electric kettle, a milk carton, tea bags, coffee bags, and mugs.

"Wow, this is organization," she said to the two men. She neatly covered the dining table with a sheet of packing paper and set the meals in front of the chairs.

Billy grinned. "It's pretty good. Anyone who works for AA knows a great deal when he sees one. No one ever leaves voluntarily. But they get more work out of us in the deal, first, because we want to keep the job, and second, because we don't have to waste time finding shops when we're on a break."

Marigold nodded. When she had an interesting task to do, she didn't like wasting time to prepare food. This system suited her down to the ground. As soon as she had finished her cup of tea and rearranged the table and chairs, she skedaddled back to the master bedroom.

Tiggy's choices were perfect. She had been doing this job since she had been given her degree in design, and she was someone Marigold wanted to learn from. Tiggy had even boxed accessories for each room, though Marigold was tentative about using them in a house that would be up for public inspection. Bearing in mind that Tiggy would know best, she placed a mirrored jewelry box on the tall dresser with a couple of framed photos of anonymous people.

She had finished styling the house when she left with the men a little after four. Tomorrow, while she researched the next job, noted in Tiggy's book as the interior design for the old school, she would begin sorting out the warehouse.

* * * *

Hagen walked into his home through the gym attached to the garage, and switched on the main lights. The soles of his shoes clipped over the white marble floor to the main hallway. He took the pristine, white-painted stairway, heading for his white bedroom, where he swapped his suit jacket for a black knit. The dull chime of the old grandfather clock downstairs was the only sound in stark silence.

He remembered all over again that he now lived alone, and that the house would remain silent—no more Mercia clattering around in the kitchen, no more Mercia opening or closing doors, turning her music up loudly, or talking to him from obscure rooms.

Sighing, he pattered down the stairs to the kitchen at the back, through a house that was set at the perfect temperature, and he strode into the stark severity of the white room. Mercia would never return to clutter the marble counter tops with her piles of food that would not be eaten before the use-by date. She liked to be prepared for any event and consistently over-catered.

He spotted his evening meal, a pasta dish of some sort, left by his daily help, who also tidied his house and ironed his shirts, except on weekends. Duly, he put the plate into the microwave, and poured himself a glass of wine.

One place had been set in the adjoining dining room, a massive space, mainly white, softened by a pale gray carpet. The biggest, whitest chandelier imaginable, bar the matching one in the entrance hall, hung over the white dining table. He sipped, the timer rang, and he carried his meal and his glass to his set place.

After he had eaten and finished his wine, Hagen strode into his study off the main hallway, a room with French doors that opened out to the side garden. He had fought with Mercia about the furnishings in this room, a Persian carpet in blue and gold, a comfortable tan leather couch, and his gigantic antique desk with a walnut patina he could never resist running a palm along. He did so again before sitting in his creaky, swiveling desk chair and checking his mail.

Mercia hadn't liked him bringing his work home, but he was the business manager of his father's large company and had been for three years, since the age of twenty-six. Rather than let the world assume he owed his position to his father, he was determined to prove he had earned his job on merit. Even now he still insisted on proving himself, and this fact wouldn't have entered his mind but for seeing Marigold Reynolds again.

Obstinate, confident Marigold with the marigold hair had grown into a wary, self-possessed woman. She hadn't lost that quick tongue of hers, but he had lost his ability to laugh. Apathy had stolen his mind, and beside her he acted slow and sluggish. Perhaps he had been that way when he had met her, over ten years ago, when Tiggy had first brought her home, but he had never taken much notice of his sisters' giggly chums.

He rested his chin on the knuckle of his fist, staring blankly at his computer screen. The summer before his last year at school—the year he had turned eighteen—he and his sisters had been allowed to invite one friend each to stay with the Allbrook family for Christmas at their beach house. He had invited Brent Adams, a member of his swimming team who was also interested in sailing. Any eighteen-year-old with two younger sisters would want to escape them for the summer, and Hagen's plan had been to set up his yacht and spend most of the days sailing with Brent. That or go surfing. Calli had invited one of her nerdy friends, and Tiggy had invited Marigold.

As soon as Brent spotted Marigold he had another plan. With her neatly contained curly red hair and her awful clothes, she looked like an easy conquest, or so Brent had said. As soon as he discovered she wasn't interested in him, he got snarky. He mumbled about her to Hagen, who wouldn't have bothered trying to change her mind the way Brent did, which was to niggle at her.

"Ignore her. She's too young anyway," Hagen had said with all the confidence of his eighteen-year-old self.

"I'll ignore her at school, that's for sure."

Hagen didn't have that luxury, since his sisters hung on her every word, but Marigold annoyed the hell out of him that summer. She had a habit of staring a challenge right into a person's eyes. Despite dressing in the charity shops' rejects, she had poise and an innate confidence he hadn't seen before in a kid her age. She knew who she was, and she didn't think much of Hagen and Brent.

And then when they got back to town, she and his sisters, then in tenth grade, had shifted into the senior school. A senior himself, he had been appointed the school captain that last year, as well as being the captain of the football team and the captain of the swimming team. Marigold joined the swimming team.

Her swimsuit was the only piece of her school uniform that suited her. Her skirts and blazers looked weary and her hems had been let down. Clearly, she wore the same uniforms from a couple of years back. His sisters had new uniforms each year as they grew. Yet again, she marked herself out as being poor. And he wouldn't have minded if she hadn't had a way of making him feel inferior.

She spoke better than he, using a drawling upper-class accent. And she threw out challenges faster than he could pick them up. Primarily, he was an athletic scholar with rich parents. She was a socially connected, scholarship student with a single mother who worked as a dental nurse. Never the twain should meet. And yet she swam like a fish on steroids. As the year progressed, her body grew curvier and her speech more diplomatic. They won the interschool championship that year. He was the golden boy, and she was a smart-mouthed sixteen-year-old.

Back then, he had tried not to notice her. However, she taught him his final lesson six years ago, which he had tried and failed to understand. Fortunately, this had motivated him to stay away from her. He didn't plan to let himself get involved with her again. She would be gone in three months, and good riddance. Meanwhile, he had schedules to plan, meetings to attend, and a whole lot of forgetting to do.

And yet, when he awoke in the morning, Marigold's presence in his workspace was the first thing to enter his mind. Tiggy had told him Marigold would be taking over for her when she had informed him she would be toddling off for three months. He should have told her to find someone else. Instead, she had left him with the only person in his life who had completely and utterly rejected him.

He arrived in the staff car park directly behind Marigold, as would naturally happen when he wanted to avoid her. He took his named spot, and she drew up in the general area. She, of course, drove a small car of obscure make. He couldn't walk off without acknowledging her and so he waited. She, of course, stared his car up and down without a word.

"I know I should drive a twenty-year-old homemade car, but I prefer speed and comfort," he said, using his bored voice.

"I didn't say a word, and if I had, it wouldn't be about your beautiful car. Don't doubt it, if I had less class and more money, I would buy one of those, too."

He blinked at her. She didn't smile but her whole face expressed hope. Her eyes sparkled and her mouth pursed. He eked out a reluctant laugh, possibly for the first time in a year or more. "Words you might wish had remained unspoken."

"Oh? Was I making one of those comments that make me sound like an envious snob?"

He put his hand to the back of his neck and considered. "That sounds like something I might once have said."

"It does, doesn't it? And I might have said something about the high proportion of village idiots who owned fast cars. But I also might have grown up a little."

"Since school days? *I know*," he said with emphasis, staring straight into her eyes. He began to walk with her to the loading bay door.

"Though I'm still wearing hand-me-downs. Well, that might change in the near future. You will be pleased to know that for three months I will be earning more than the average wage. I might even buy something smart."

He glanced back at her, concentrating for the first time on the clothes she wore. If they were hand-me-downs, he wouldn't have guessed, not that she wore the type of clothes Mercia used to buy, which he knew were expensive and seen only a few times before she loaded her dressing room with her next buys. Marigold wore a plain blue shirt with a black skirt and jacket. She looked like any businesswoman of his acquaintance, except for her light golden-red hair, which she had tangled into a knot at the back of her head. As ever, the soft curly tendrils around her face had escaped. He thought she didn't wear much makeup. Her eyelashes, long and spiky, seemed to be her own, but what would he know? "How did you manage yesterday?"

"Pretty well, I think, but Tiggy had everything organized for me. I see the next on the list is to design the interior of a building that has been renovated for sale. I gather I decide which style."

He nodded. "Based on the area and the age of the building, though not necessarily. For example, I have an old house, but my wife wanted a modern interior." Whatever he had planned to say next didn't eventuate when he noted her wary gaze.

"I'm sure it's very beautiful."

"Most people think so." He stiffened his shoulders. "She's dead. My wife," he said, wishing he hadn't felt the need to explain a fact that Marigold doubtlessly knew. "A car accident."

She nodded. "I know it's hard. My mother died a year ago, and I have only recently thought about having her room painted. It seemed sacrilege to wipe out memories of her with a paint color. But in the end, a room is only a room and she would have liked another color if she had lived."

"Does that mean you are alone now? I recall you didn't have much to do with your father."

"Or my half brothers." She made a wry face. "They went to our school, you know, but they were in the junior school while I was in the senior school so I hardly ever saw them. Once my father had sons, he was happy to forget his daughter existed."

He already knew that she had younger brothers who barely knew her and a father who chose not to. Hagen might have attitude himself if either of his parents had been so uncaring. Instead he had a bright mother, a somewhat severe but loving father, and two smart sisters. He had based his later reactions toward Marigold on his mistaken assumption that he was one of life's winners, but he doubted that any other hormonally driven bonehead would have been any more sensitive to the nuances than he. He needed to think of himself less often rather than think less of himself.

He parted from her at his office door, realizing that his tone when he mentioned his house must have given her a hint that he didn't admire the modern décor; the cold, impersonal, disposable furnishings; and Mercia's deliberately conspicuous spending. As soon as he could motivate himself, he had every intention of wiping out the memory of her with a change.

The only room he liked was his study.

Chapter 2

Marigold wandered into the workroom glad that she and Hagen had made peace at last. The unspoken issue between them had lurked for six years. *I know.* Naturally she was never going to apologize for pricking his male ego, but at the time she had hurt herself as well. She'd had no choice.

Now that he had also been hit with the reality of life and death, and he quite clearly suffered the loss of his wife, she experienced a tad of contrition. From now on, she would treat him with the respect any boss would expect from an employee.

With a release of pent-up breath, she sat at Tiggy's desk and fingered the notebook clearly meant for her. The cover had been illustrated with a garish orange pencil drawing of a flower, which looked roughly like a marigold, but the best hint was "Marigold" written with a black marker pen. She smiled and moved the pad aside, glancing at the paint cards, color swatches, scraps of paper, pencils, pens, a length of black ribbon, two feathers, a packet of mints, a scalpel, a pencil sharpener, and a desk calendar. Okay, all were essential items, but not on a working space. Tiggy had left this in as great a mess as the furniture bay.

Before Marigold could begin, she needed to make Tiggy's desk into her own: neat and tidy. She opened the top drawer, noted a caddy, and she dropped the pens, pencils, sharpener, and scalpel on top. Paper and notebooks appeared to belong in the second drawer, and everything else went into the bottom drawer, whether it belonged there or not.

Now, with her desk space free, she scanned the rest of the room—the rolls of fabric, the cushion innards, a box of curtain tie backs, various handles, and door fittings. A few small articles had no particular meaning at this time, like a stack of old books, multicolored small boxes, and a plant stand. She would find a plant for the stand and take the rest to the warehouse.

Now she could start work. Setting the Marigold notebook in front of her, she flipped through pages of numbers, addresses, and doodles until she came to the last. Here, Tiggy had itemized tasks headed The Schoolhouse.

1. Kell will drop in sometime on Tuesday afternoon and drive you to the schoolhouse.

2. Take color swatches and paint cards.

Even for Tiggy, that was taking brevity a little too far. Marigold had never designed the innards of a house before. A hint or two would have been appreciated. Sighing, she took the articles out of the bottom drawer and dropped them into her bag, with a handful of pencils and a notebook, in fact, most of the things she had recently put away. She thought about adding the feather and the mints, but decided she could risk having neither of those handy during a house inspection.

Since she saw no place for the rolls of fabric in the office, she managed the three of them all the way along the passage to the warehouse without any slipping from her grip. She used her foot to pry open the connecting door to the warehouse. As she dropped the rolls with a stack of others, a shadow crossed the doorway.

She turned, noting a glamorous young woman dressed in a delicious red floral dress and red high heels.

"Knock, knock," the woman said as she stepped inside the doorway. After lifting her ombre blond hair to one shoulder, she rehooked the straps of her expensive multicolored leather bag onto her shoulder. "What a ghastly day. Is Tiggy here?" Her smooth face barely creased with her smile.

"She won't be back for another three months. I'm Marigold. I've taken over Tiggy's job in the meantime."

"How nice to meet you, Marigold. Such a sweet old-fashioned name. I'm Scarlett, and I'm a friend of the Allbrooks, here on a charity mission. The Adelaide Dramatic Society needs a few props for their latest show. I believe the society has borrowed Allbrook's staging furniture from time to time. They need a three-seater blue couch for their latest production, or so the set designer said. Do you have one?" Scarlett's perfectly drawn eyebrows queried Marigold.

Smiling politely, Marigold offered a rueful shrug. "I'm not sure I have the authority to give you furniture. If you don't mind waiting for a few minutes, I'll ask Hagen."

Scarlett looked amused. "Hagen won't mind. We're very good friends."

Marigold didn't doubt that for one moment. Scarlett was Hagen's type—polished, manicured, and shiny new. "I'll just check with him."

"I'll come with you."

"Please do." With Scarlett striding behind her, Marigold led the way to the office block and then to Hagen's suite. "Is Hagen available?" she asked Sandra.

Sandra glanced at Scarlett. "Mrs. Haines, good morning. Yes, Hagen is in." Scarlett moved in front of Marigold and opened the door of Hagen's office. "Hagen, darling," she said and she closed the door behind her.

"Oops," Marigold said blinking at Sandra. "She wanted to borrow furniture, and I wasn't sure who she was."

"She was a friend of his wife. She broke up with her husband last year, which might be significant. Or not." Sandra kept her voice low, staring at the door. "I wonder why she wants to borrow furniture?"

"For The Adelaide Dramatic Society," she said.

"Oh. Tiggy usually lets theater companies borrow whatever they want, but I didn't know Mrs. Haines had any connection there."

"She said something about a charity call. I hope Hagen doesn't mind having his day interrupted by this."

"If you were a man would you mind being confronted with Mrs. Haines in the morning?"

Marigold laughed. "I see your point. Well, I'll get back to whatever I was doing."

In less than five minutes, while Marigold was finding a place for a set of glass vases, which meant she had to find another space for three porcelain bowls, Scarlett returned with Hagen, who looked slightly ruffled. "Give Scarlett whatever she wants," he said to Marigold. "I must get back to work."

"You're a sweetheart, Hagen." Scarlett rested her red fingernails on Hagen's wide shoulder, and stood on her toes to give him a lingering kiss near his mouth.

His hand briefly touched her arm. "Marigold will help you."

Scarlett's gaze hooded. "Oh, yes. Marigold." She stood, watching him leave. Most women would. Then she turned to Marigold, appearing politely bored. "A blue three-seater couch?"

"Right. This way. Follow me."

Scarlett followed Marigold up and down the aisles while she peeked under dust sheets trying to find what the other woman wanted. "Here's one." She stopped at a navy-blue couch.

"That will be perfect. Can your man deliver it today?"

"My man?"

"I was told you had a man to do your deliveries," Scarlett said with an imperious frown.

Not at all eager to ask Hagen another officious question, Marigold nodded. "We have a delivery team. I'll see when Billy can deliver."

"The company will be finished with the couch in three weeks, they told me. You can get your man to pick it up then. Thank you, Muriel. I'll tell Hagen how helpful you've been."

Trying to look like a Muriel, Marigold squeezed out a smile but she doubted Hagen would care to hear about her usefulness. He expected her to do as she was told, and she would, for three months.

She couldn't find Billy or Joe, but determined to save them work, she scraped the couch over to the loading bay doors. Finding the furniture for Scarlett wasn't a waste of time, because she had discovered AA & Co. supported amateur theater productions, a generosity she admired. Without the local productions, young actors wouldn't have a chance, and many professional actors wouldn't be able to pay back the start they had received themselves. Nor would hopeful young set designers have the opportunity to show their talents.

Plus, Marigold had found a kind of method in Tiggy's madness. Tiggy put any old couch of any old size or color in the aisle nearest to the loading bay, clearly because these were the heaviest articles. The matching armchairs occupied the middle of the same aisle. Single chairs sat at the far end. Tables of all sizes filled the next row. Wardrobes were rare, but those AA owned were antiques and set against the back wall.

Now that Marigold knew the system, she emptied the boxes, and placed the smaller props—the vases, the cups and saucers, the plates, an umbrella, suitcases, and what-all—on various shelves. Dusting off her hands, she strolled to the staff cafeteria, not only for a coffee but hoping to spot Billy.

Instead she saw Hagen select a mug from the overhead shelves and turn to the coffee machine.

"Could you tell me where Billy might be at this time of day?" she asked him with her best professional smile.

He glanced at her. "He and Joe are at Kell's workshop. They have a kitchen to pick up and deliver. Why?"

"I need them to deliver the couch we've loaned to The Adelaide Dramatic Society for their latest show."

"Why are we delivering the couch?"

"Scarlett implied that we deliver and pick up." An element of nervousness lowered her tone.

He frowned. "We let the companies borrow items, but they are supposed to arrange for the collections and returns themselves."

Marigold swallowed. Her chest deflated. "So, will I have to tell her that we won't deliver and pick up?"

"That would be unfair, wouldn't it, when she probably enjoyed conning you?" He dropped a pod into the coffee machine.

"So, I've been caught in a charity scam." Marigold made a deliberately exaggerated face of self-disgust. "I should have realized that beneath that highly polished exterior lurked a devious Miss Marple."

He examined her expression with eyes as blue and clear as the summer sea. "Treasure the moment. Not too many people would have seen Scarlett touting for charity." He watched the coffee drizzling into his cup. "Who's Miss Marple?"

Marigold cleared her throat, reluctant to admit to watching daytime TV to a man who probably watched the news, at best. "A television detective. She acts like a doddering little old lady and no one recognizes the sharp mind behind her sweet face. Scarlett looks like…well, you know what she looks like."

"She looks like my late wife, except for the color of her hair." His lips clamped.

She huffed out a slow breath. "That must be hard. Every reminder is hard. We like to pretend they can come back and watch over us while we know they can't." Her eyes prickled. Talking about her dead mother to anyone who hadn't suffered a loss was like talking to a sympathetic brick wall. Those people assumed that mourning the loss of a loved one had a use-by date.

"I'm sorry about your mother." A muscle in his jaw ticked as he glanced at her. "Was her death sudden?"

She glanced away. He didn't know about her mother's condition and he hadn't been notified about her death. Either Tiggy or Calli must have told him. "She'd been ill for some time. I have accepted that I'll grieve forever without being in mourning forever. It's harder for you." She indicated that his cup had filled.

He nodded briefly, showing he understood, which of course he did, although the shock of losing a young healthy wife was likely far more difficult than watching the suffering of a loved mother end. "I'll get Billy to deliver whatever she wants as soon as he can." He pressed the stop button and courteously passed his coffee to her.

"Thank you. And, in future I'll watch glamorous women with appealing smiles a little more carefully." She added milk to the cup, while he started another for himself.

"I don't intend to micromanage," he said, concentrating on the coffee stream, "but we don't let many people borrow our props. I'm surprised Tiggy didn't mention this. I'll leave you to decide who can, based on something other than glamour."

"Driver's license?"

He gave her a sideways glance and stalked off.

She didn't know what to make of Hagen these days, though the death of his wife would have woken him up to the fact that life was short. In his own distant way, he was kind. She couldn't say the same about him during their school days. His deliberate ignore of her back then had made an impact on a girl who was well aware that everyone knew her mother bought her school uniforms secondhand. This wasn't necessarily unusual in a school that charged exorbitant fees, but she was a friend of his sisters, and he saw her in his home at least once a week. He could easily have been a lot friendlier.

Added to that, in his last year Hagen had been the bleeding, bloody captain of everything, the school, the football team, and the swimming team. One thing she had been really good at was swimming. He absolutely hadn't looked at her during training, and she'd been certain he wouldn't select her for the inter-schools' team, but in the end he had to because she had beaten every other girl in the school. She had tried to approach him about her position on the relay team, and he'd said, "Get dressed."

Get dressed? Every other person on the team could talk to him wearing a swimsuit, but she had to get dressed? He didn't tell his girlfriend to get dressed, and she had the biggest breasts in the school, and she wobbled them under everyone's nose. Marigold liked her body, which wasn't excessive. The only person on the swimming team she would tell to get dressed was bleeding, bloody Brent, who already had the beginnings of a potbelly at the age of eighteen. Who wanted to see that?

In retrospect, Hagen looked fabulous in his swimmers, showing most of his golden-tanned, tall, muscular body. Girls tended to approach him wearing as little as possible, in the hope of his attention for reasons other than wanting to swim last in the relay. He probably thought she was trying the same thing, but as a friend of his sisters that would be low, and probably hurt the most, knowing he thought she had been interested in throwing herself at him. Bigheaded jerk.

But that was then. Time had passed and the few memorable occasions they'd met since schooldays had been put to the back of her mind. Easing her shoulders, again she stared at the sweet treats in the servery and again she deprived herself in favor of getting back to the restacking of the warehouse.

Billy arrived about an hour later, and he shook his head over the delivery to the theater's backstage. "If I had known this morning, I could have done it then." He grumped off.

Marigold ate her lunch in guilty silence, and then she shifted various chairs around the warehouse. Although any good designer would hear the word 'schoolhouse' and instantly see a theme, she was having an attack of procrastination. Perhaps when she saw the schoolhouse, an idea for the color scheme would waft out of the walls and inspire her. In the meantime, she had looked at new bathrooms online until her eyes ached. She needed shortcuts in this eclectic job she had no idea how to manage. Finally, Kell, Calli Allbrook's husband, found her.

"Ready?" He waited for her to collect her bag. Kell was a man about the same height as Hagen but there the resemblance ended. Kell had dark hair and the sort of rough handsomeness that model agencies grabbed with both hands. The man was perfect for Calli, Tiggy's twin, and a quiet and contemplative woman who thought so long before she spoke that mainly she ended up being tactful. She had been the same as a girl, careful, and everyone's idea of a thoroughly nice person.

Marigold guessed that Kell was less tactful and far more determined to have his way. His dark good looks used to intimidate her, but now she saw more than his looks. He was ultra-smart and had recently been appointed the project manager of AA by his father-in-law, Alex Allbrook, the general manager of the company, the son of the original founder, Hagen's grandfather.

When she arrived back, Kell walked her to his work vehicle, a white pickup bearing the company's logo. Within ten minutes, Kell unlocked the safety door of the main building of a former primary school. "We've got the walls up in this building, which will be converted into a duplex. We'll want your interior design by the end of the week." He followed her into the hallway.

"Right," she said, swallowing.

"We'll do the other buildings later. This is intended to be a two-stage job. As you can see, we have subdivided the site into sixteen lots. The other three buildings left standing will be converted into separate houses. The former gymnasium will have another story added and will end up being single-bedroom apartments. Student accommodation, most likely. Then we'll build ten new houses on the other lots. I have the architect's floor plans for each, and I'll give you a copy."

"When are you completing the build?"

"We're playing this one by ear, so far, doing the whole thing piecemeal. Most of the men are working on the apartment block we're building in the city, and they'll be deployed whenever they have time."

She stared at him. "Am I doing a separate design plan for each building?"

"You or Tiggy, eventually, but the school building needs to go ahead first. We want it done and sold. Alex likes to keep the money moving."

Patting her chest as though she had warded off a heart attack, she smiled with overdone relief. "Do you want the same look for both sides of the duplex?"

He shook his head. "Not necessarily the same, but similar."

Marigold checked each of the rooms, taking photos on her phone. She made notes about the windows and the sunlight as she went. Kell busied himself, but he appeared to be checking measurements rather than plotting. When Marigold indicated that she had enough information, he drove her back to AA. Before he disappeared again, he said, "I almost forgot, Calli wants me to ask you to come to dinner on Friday night."

"I would be delighted."

Then she went back to her office, and sat at her desk with a scale graph of two completely different sized bathrooms. For the next two hours, she went online to make her final choice of baths and vanities. She matched virtual tiles, and then shifted handmade cutouts around on her scale drawing of the plan until she was satisfied she had left enough room for towel rails and a double vanity.

Hagen's light shone through the crack beneath his door, but she didn't see him either come or go. Sandra spent more time away from her desk than Marigold had imagined a personal assistant would, and Hagen spent more time out of his office than in it. Likely she would too once she had worked out her routine.

She wondered if she was up to the task. For her sort of property designing while she stayed at home looking after her mother, she saved on costs wherever she could. Often, simply moving items around or into different rooms made the house look larger or smarter. If she needed a little extra padding, she knew a secondhand furniture dealer who allowed her to borrow his furniture for a tiny fee. She wasn't above making new cushion covers or finding prints to frame cheaply, either.

For AA & Co., she started from scratch. She hadn't ever been expected to plot out where a fridge would best fit into a new kitchen, though she had certainly shifted a few in old kitchens. Although she could work out all the details given time, compared to a professional like Tiggy, Marigold was a rank amateur. The scary part was that Kell's team would be making cabinets to fit her specifications. If she made a mistake, she would create extra work and costs. Aside from that, because she worked with whatever articles her private clients already owned, she had no idea of the most saleable colors for new builds.

She collected Tiggy's pile of design magazines and began skimming through, but she truly couldn't imagine living with a red kitchen for longer than a year, despite the eye-catching color. Then again, some people lived whole lifetimes surrounded by appalling colors without making any change.

She sighed. The kitchen cupboards in her mother's post-war house, now hers, were crafted from painted wood with cream laminate countertops. The house had been built in the seventies, and the kitchen had never been renewed. Most of the hinges on the cabinets had rusted and almost all hung enough askew, making closing the doors difficult. If she had the money... But she didn't.

Instead, she could enjoy renewing the old school with a modern, but not too glamorous kitchen. Built after the Second World War, 1940-ish, the severity of the architecture and the stark lines of the crown molding would be set off nicely by a modern industrial design.

She left at six and noted Hagen's car was one of the few left in the lot. Since she was supposed to report any problems to him, she decided to make tentative plans and run them by Calli when she saw her on Friday night.

* * * *

Hagen ended his last meeting at seven and drove home to his sterile house. He zapped his meal, wrote up the minutes of the last meeting of the board, and signed a pile of checks. Sandra had noted in his planner that his car was due for a service and that his sister Calli wanted him to come for dinner on Friday night. She could have called him, but he had a habit of ignoring personal phone calls, and so, like many others, she often used Sandra to keep him up to date.

Finally, he decided that an evening with her and Kell would suit him well enough. He would be sure of not eating another microwave meal, at least. He contacted Calli and accepted the invitation for seven on Friday night. A family meal wouldn't leave him wondering where the past year had gone.

* * * *

He almost forgot about Marigold, and when he saw her in the staff room on Thursday he took a step backward. Today she wore her tailored black pants and a crisp white shirt. Her beautiful hair had been swirled on top of her head.

"Good morning," she said with one of her classy smiles.

He nodded. "Morning. How's the job going?"

"The schoolhouse? It's not as easy to plot what goes where as you might think."

As the person who had plotted 'what goes where' in his first year with his father's company, he tried a sympathetic shift of his mouth. "Computer modeling helps."

"But first you need to know the size of the loo and the bath, and how much space you need to take a shower."

"Surely the sizes would be on the computer program?" He glanced over at the far table where the company's architect sat with the building foreman, planning to join them.

Her jaw moved a little to the side as she thought. "I hope not since I spent hours finding the specifications online."

"Didn't Tiggy run through all that with you?" Unlike most redheads he knew, Marigold had dark eyelashes. Her eyes were the color of a fine old brandy—big, candid, beautiful eyes, glossed with health.

She blinked and a slight crease formed between her delicate eyebrows. "She told me she didn't use the computer often, but I might find something useful. If so, I don't know what or where."

He edged sideways, wanting his employees to note that he wouldn't spend too much time in conversation with an attractive woman. A man whose wife had recently died had to mourn: needed to respect her memory. "So, you're reinventing the wheel."

"You could say that." She lifted her shoulders.

"You ought to have told me you were having a problem." He glanced away, frustrated. She shouldn't be in this position that was clearly out of her depth. Tiggy had insisted that Marigold could handle a job that depended on more than the color of a few tiles, and he didn't know why Tiggy had chosen her if she couldn't easily knock off a design for an interior. He hoped she could coordinate events because that would be her main role, in his opinion. The designing was important, but impressing prospective clients was more important. Mercia had had the knack. Marigold was as yet, untried.

"I probably don't like showing my ignorance. In my normal line of work, I only use a computer to order or find materials."

Although he knew he should sit at one of the tables with her and sort out her problems, he couldn't handle too much time with Marigold. The sight of her squeezed at his insides and reminded him of that night during his final year at university when he had made an irretrievable mistake. "Sandra will help you," he said, backing out of the room, coffee in hand, instead of joining the builder and the architect.

He shouldn't have allowed Marigold to interrupt his disciplined routine. After super-efficient, slightly motherly Sandra had spoken to Marigold, his PA entered his office, her forehead creased. "She's right. Tiggy left her out on a limb. She doesn't have any sort of list of the projects or the specs. I'm going to send her everything. In the meantime, she has done color swatches, etcetera. Nice job, too."

He sent a text message to Tiggy. *What's up? Why did you leave Marigold hung out to dry?*

No answer, but he could see she read the message. Perhaps Marigold and Tiggy had had a falling out. Hagen had never known either of his sisters to be spiteful. He still hadn't heard from Tiggy by the time he pulled up outside Calli's house on Friday night. Another car sat right outside the front gate of the place Calli and Kell were currently renovating. Marigold's blue car.

He gripped his steering wheel. The thought of Kell and Calli having a dinner guest other than him hadn't entered his head. Finally, he stalked up the garden path, stepped onto the slatted veranda, and rang the doorbell. A couple of light footsteps and Kell, dressed in jeans and a woolly sweater, opened the door.

"I thought this was a family meal?" Hagen said in an accusing voice. He pushed a bottle of red wine at Kell's chest.

"You saw Marigold's car? She is family, according to Calli." Kell led the way to the open plan living area.

Calli had chosen plain white walls for the seventies house. Light, polished hardwood flooring connected the kitchen, the dining room, and the sitting room where a dark blue carpet square complemented the mellow wood. Pops of primary colors had been added in the pictures on the walls and other than that, his youngest sister had furnished in contemporary style.

"Nice," he said, glancing around. He hadn't been in this house before and he knew Kell and Calli would make quite a few dollars when Kell sold the place on, which was his intention. Living off his wife's money didn't suit him, being the proud and independent type.

Hagen understood, although he hadn't been brought up poor. He had insisted on paying for his own house, too, despite his father's impatience. "It will be yours anyway, so why not spend some now?" Far had said, but Hagen didn't want a house he would sell on. He wanted a lifetime house, one in which his children would flourish. But he didn't have children, and he no longer had a wife.

He pushed his hands into his pockets and glanced over to the kitchen where Marigold and Calli stood, the latter grinning at him and accepting the bottle of wine from Kell. Calli was tall and elegant with dark hair like their mother. She had the light eyes they had all inherited from Far. The only difference between Calli and Tiggy was their hair color, which changed on a whim. Both had inherited Ma's cooking skills, but Calli pretended she was a novice, a ploy that had Ma, but no one else, fooled. Ma continued to bury Calli under mountains of food offerings. She had stopped her food parcels to Hagen not long after he married Mercia. No doubt she assumed Mercia had inherited her mother's cooking skills.

He smiled at Calli, and flickered his gaze to Marigold. "Nice to see you again, Marigold," he said, folding his arms across his chest, a challenging stance that appalled him. Gazing at his feet, he switched his hands back to his pockets, trying to appear casual but in a room with Marigold, he felt anything but casual.

He had no idea why she always looked right for every occasion without appearing to try, but tonight she wore those plain black pants with a pale blue knitted top. Her beautiful shiny hair had been straightened and fell to her shoulders in a glimmer of gold. Tonight would be unbearable.

Marigold offered a pasted smile. "After all this time?" Her glance at him expressed the vague amusement of the unreadable younger woman she had been.

"A whole day." He could have bitten his tongue. He hadn't meant to sound as though he noticed. "We're not going to talk about work, I hope," he said, clamping his jaw.

"What if it finds its way into the conversation?"

He sighed. Irrepressible Marigold. Again, she had left him without a comeback. He glanced at Kell, who said, "Would you like a beer or a glass of your wine?"

"Whatever you like."

Kell gave him beer. The conversation drifted into talk of food while the ladies nursed a glass of wine each. After pulling warm plates from the oven, Calli asked them to sit at the table. Hagen sat opposite Marigold, who spread her table napkin on her lap without glancing at him. He did the same while Calli served apple and pumpkin soup. The delicately sweet flavor caught at his taste buds.

For the past year, he had avoided family meals. He didn't want the sympathy he didn't deserve, preferring to wallow in his wretchedness.

Tonight, the clear bright colors in the room, the fragrant food, and the sheer pleasure of gazing at calm and careful Marigold relaxed him.

He savored a lamb roast with crisp roasted vegetables, and a pastry packed with creamy custard drizzled with honey syrup. He rarely ate sweets—the decision of the athlete he no longer was, but tonight he wanted everything he had missed. Yes, even Marigold. Marigold most. She had a swimmer's body, fit and healthy, that he would appreciate in his bed, and graceful hands that he could easily imagine caressing his needy body.

At the moment, her hands rested idly on the table. He groaned silently, feeling the rush of blood to his dick. After lighthearted small talk, while he tried to concentrate on the words rather than Marigold, the company relaxed on the L-shaped sofa. Calli curled against Kell. The pretty little cat they had acquired sat along the top of the couch, every now and again batting at Kell's face to encourage his attention.

"Remember that summer we spent at Goolwa?" Calli said, idly toying with one of Kell's fingers.

Hagen knew which summer she meant because she included Marigold in her gaze. "We spent most summers at Goolwa," he said, hoping to change the subject. He had enough problems with Marigold sitting only an angle away.

"I'm talking about the summer before Tiggy and I moved into the senior school. Marigold was with us for Christmas. I love big family Christmases. We haven't had one for ages. Kell and I are thinking of going to Goolwa with Ma and Far this year."

"Do you sail, Kell?"

Kell shook his head and dragged the cat onto his lap.

Calli answered for him. "Kell isn't a beach boy like you."

"I'll bet he plays a mean game of volleyball."

Kell grinned. "Mean is the word. I have two brothers. If you come, too, I'll challenge you to a Dee-style game. We play by rules decided on by what the women are wearing."

Hagen scratched the back of his neck. "Whatever floats your boat. Speaking of which, if I come, I'll take you out sailing."

"We blessed your sailing that year. We got rid of handy ol' Brent for a while." Marigold gleamed a smile at him. "Handy as in, my god, he was a grabber, wasn't he Calli?"

"You got the worst of it. I think he was a bit scared of touching Hagen's sisters."

Hagen glanced at Marigold. His neck tightened. "If he was touching you, you should have said something."

"I thought I dealt with him quite well. I touched him back, tweaked him actually, and it hurt. It might have given him the idea that grabbing a girl's breasts hurt, too. Anyway, he didn't speak to me again, even at school. I see he married Dina Douglas, aka Dido."

"How do you know that?"

"I saw it in the paper a couple of years ago. It's a shame you grabbed her back then, because if he could have had her, it would have taken the pressure off the rest of us." Marigold laughed, and her eyes crinkled with mischief.

"If only you had asked me back then, I would have thrown her to the wolf," Hagen answered with intentional sarcasm. He didn't want to want Marigold. "No sacrifice would have been too great for you."

"It's a shame that's past tense because in the present I'm tense. I see in the notes Tiggy left for me that I'm supposed to be organizing a dinner for you next Friday. Why do you need me to organize a dinner for you? Surely it's only a matter of calling a restaurant and if you can't do that, Sandra could."

He glanced at Calli who moistened her lips before she spoke. "Tiggy's been organizing Hagen's business dinners since Mercia died. Mercia used to handle the social aspect, and Tiggy managed the organizational part."

"What part is the organizational part?" Marigold stared straight at him. He shrugged. "Invitations, table decorations."

"He thinks it's that easy," Calli said, shaking her head. "For an intimate dinner, you need to know the invitees nationalities and their dietary requirements. You might want place cards, name cards. For a larger dinner, you might want a speaker, an order of speaking, sponsors, entertainment. The list goes on. Sometimes you might want a red carpet or photographers, or even the media."

"Not for this dinner," Hagen said, alarmed. "I'll be hosting it at home."

"In your house?"

"Home is what I call my house."

"So, I'm organizing a dinner in your home?"

"Imagine it's a restaurant."

"Dinner for how many?"

Hagen frowned, again puzzled. "Tiggy must have left you instructions."

"It said in the notebook, and I quote, 'Organize Hagen's dinner.'"

"Perhaps Sandra knows the details."

"If it's in your house, you'll need what? A caterer and staff?"

"You can get the caterer to supply staff." Calli glanced at Hagen. "Hagen, stop being unhelpful. All of this must have been booked weeks ago."

"Yes. I'm sure it was. I recall Tiggy saying everyone accepted."

Marigold breathed out. "Good. So, everyone will arrive, and presumably to have accepted, they'll know where to go. At worst, I'll only need to run around like a headless chicken trying to organize a caterer for X number of people with various food intolerances. At best, that's done, and Sandra knows the arrangement."

"And the hours you spend at my house will be paid at double time, if that makes this more palatable." He glanced at Marigold's expression, which he couldn't read, had never been able to read, and he wondered if that was her attraction. Mercia's face had always warned him about what she was about to say or do, but he had never fathomed Marigold.

"I'll be at your house?"

He spread his hands. "You're Tiggy's stand-in. For the past year, she has been my hostess. That's why she wanted you for this job—you're not a stranger to me."

She sat with her hands in her lap, the irises in her big brandy-colored eyes huge. "That does it. I'll have to buy a new dress."

She smiled at him, and old memories of her smart, wryly funny words flooded his mind. He concentrated on the coffee table in front of him, anything but think about her.

A man would be a fool to want a woman he couldn't have. Aside from that, he didn't deserve another chance.

Chapter 3

Marigold dealt with her usual Saturday morning chores—a load of washing, vacuuming the house, and driving off for her week's food supply. At the shopping center, she filled her car with her normal boring staples. Then, resigned to her least favorite task, she took the escalator from the car park back into the mall.

Now spring had begun to warm into summer, the new summer fashions crowded the shops. The older spring fashions were being price-dumped. At a discount of at least fifty percent, she could buy a new dress to wear to Hagen's dinner. Since she would mainly be background noise, black would be her choice. To find the best bargain, she started at the supermarket end of the mall and skimmed the discounted racks in each boutique along the strip. Apparently black was passé this year, but farther down the mall, she found a straight gray-and-black dress with three-quarter sleeves. She took that for fifty dollars, reduced from two hundred and thirty.

As she triumphantly swung her designer-labeled package to the escalator, she spotted Hagen standing near the flower shop. Her heartbeat skittered. She wore jeans, a sweater, and flat-heeled boat shoes and with her hair flying around her face, she looked like a housewife who was returning home to unpack her groceries. He wore jeans and a cream knit. He looked tall, blond, and tanned, like a fairytale prince slumming.

As if he sensed her desperation not to be seen, he turned his head. His hesitant smile showed a glimpse of his perfect white teeth. With no obvious choice, she continued walking toward him, her breath regrettably short. His height and his coloring separated him from the crowd of busy shoppers. She hoped he saw her polite smile and not the smile of a star-struck minion. Last night, she'd had a normal conversation with him, one that hadn't left him tight-lipped.

Stopping in front of him, she clutched her bag to her chest her, trying desperately to meet his careful gaze. "I've shopped in the same place for most of my life, and I have seen most of the people I know in this particular mall at some time, but this is weird so soon after last night." She moved into an awkward hip-shot stance.

He nodded, as cool and calm as he had always been. "That's so, bearing in mind that shopping is not one of my hobbies. Are you leaving now, or do you have time for a coffee with me?" His eyes met hers and her body jolted into shocking sexual awareness.

Until last night she hadn't had a real conversation with him for six years. "Since we've never managed that at work, why not? We ought to talk about this dinner of yours."

"Yes, we ought to."

She could tell herself as often as she liked that he was not for her, but she'd been helplessly attracted to him from the first time she had slipped into a seat at his parents' table for a meal. Perhaps part of his attraction stemmed from the fact that he was her weak, indecisive father's polar opposite. Hagen had always known where he was going, and nothing could have been clearer than that he would take a glamorous woman like Mercia with him.

"Which coffee place do you prefer?" he asked, his gaze piercing through her.

Once upon a time, she had thought she could read the expression in his eyes, but that turned out to be a self-delusion. "Since you're not a regular here, you might not know the best place to buy a lemon curd tart, so follow me."

He didn't quite follow her, instead choosing to walk beside her, and she paced along in princess mode. Being with a good-looking man did that to a woman, and she noted how many other women glanced at him as he passed by. At the nicest, quietest coffee shop, he pulled out a chair for her and he ordered her coffee at the counter without asking what she wanted. Apparently he had noted previously, which was the sort of impressive thing Hagen did. He also bought two lemon curd tarts, and she blessed her hinting skills.

"Do you have a large kitchen to prepare food?" she asked as he placed the treats on the table.

"Yes."

"Will I need to hire plates?"

"No."

"Why isn't your mother doing this meal? She's the wife of the managing director of the company, and she's a wonderful caterer. She's done huge parties with only the help of her aunties. You know I know that."

He shrugged. "Her aunties are in their eighties, and Ma says she is tired. She thinks it's time for the younger generation to take over. Or, was that a trick question?"

"Hagen, your mother knows Mercia is no longer around," she said using a patient tone. Sympathy wouldn't help him in the least. She didn't know what would, but her being in Mercia's house would be awkward. "I'm sure she would help if she were asked."

He shook his head. "I wouldn't ask. Mercia took over the moment she married me, and Ma stepped out then. Fair enough."

"So, Tiggy and you often do these things?"

"We use my house only when the list is under twelve people and comprises people we would like to be…" Clearly measuring his words, he pulled his ear lobe, and drew his eyebrows together. "In our more intimate group. People who wouldn't necessarily be impressed by an expensive venue, but might be with a more intimate style."

"You mean by the family silverware?"

"So to speak."

"Do you have the silverware?"

"Mercia made sure of that." His mouth lifted at one corner.

She leaned her chin into her palm, her gaze catching his. "So, you want something classy for the decorations."

He blinked and nodded. "I looked at the details of the dinner last night after I arrived home. I'm expecting two politicians with wives, a couple of people from the university, my parents, you, and me. And someone from the government, with partner."

"That's going to be cozy," she said, trying to suppress a laugh. "Not. Do you have a log fire?"

He gave her a quelling glance, shook his head, and picked up his tart. "My house isn't cozy. This is tasty," he said, after his first bite. "I can see why you wanted to come here. Are you busy today?"

"As busy as every Saturday," she said with an amount of defensiveness. She would have liked to sound as if she had a full social calendar but she only had chores, chores, and chores.

"What about if we have lunch at my house? You could look over the place instead of asking questions that I might not be satisfactorily answering."

"I have to unpack my shopping and do all sorts other things." She frowned at him.

"What other things? Anything you can't put off?"

She tried to consider while she ate a couple of bites of her tart, but because of his wife's untimely death, she had to harden herself to the fact she would have to see him in the intimate surrounding of the house he had lived in with wonderful, efficient, perfect Mercia. "Okay. We may as well get it over with."

"Lunch might be good." He leaned back, his eyebrows raised, assessing the cost of her outfit, for all she knew.

"What are you offering?"

He did one of those Hagen smiles that made his eyes gleam and his hard mouth soften. "I'll buy something here. What do you recommend?"

"You can't ask someone for lunch, tell them it might be good, and then get them to decide on the menu," she said, unwillingly charmed by his attempt to bribe her with food.

His head inclined slightly to the side. "I'm perfectly happy to accommodate your tastes."

"You're perfectly happy to get your own way." She remembered this about him all too well, but she also remembered the ease with which they used to converse. Easy companionship with a man was rare for her. The male members of her family treated her like a poor relation. Hagen had always treated her like an intelligent person. She breathed out. "And I'm perfectly happy with a sandwich for lunch. Write out your address, and I'll be there at one." After he had gone, and while she was brushing crumbs off her mouth, she stared at the card he had left with her.

He lived within walking distance of her house.

* * * *

Hagen had bought a selection of mixed sandwiches and a box of sweet pastries and dumped the lot on the marble counter top in the kitchen, along with a loaf of rye bread and a dozen eggs. He should have bought flowers. Mercia disliked anything other than formal arrangements in the house, but his mother used anything she had in the garden and that gave the sort of cheer he needed in his empty rooms.

Mercia always had guests, too, especially on weekends. Since she had died, he had used weekends for catching up on work or for driving down to the coast and staring at the sea. He didn't do either while Mercia was alive. She had a full social calendar that included him. On Saturday mornings, she would dash off to the supermarket to pick up last minute items she had decided she needed. Perpetually disorganized, she would unpack her endless groceries while mumbling about tradesmen she wanted him to deal with. "They don't listen to a woman."

Then later, he would find people had been invited around for a game of tennis, code for sitting around the pool and drinking. When the crowds inevitably dispersed, he would be let off the hook long enough to change for a social event, where he would donate money or patronage to a worthy cause, and he would be moving from foot to foot while Mercia gossiped about who was sleeping with whom—in the midst of her shiny friends, most of whom had hinted they could make themselves available to him, had he crooked a finger.

Mercia had been his perfect partner, like him the third generation of her family to live in Australia. Her grandparents, like his, had arrived after the war and had started a market garden, a business that grew. Her parents had been the first generation to be university educated, like his, and had expanded the original thriving business into a multi-million-dollar empire, the same as his parents had done. She, like him, had benefited.

Even after her marriage, her parents continued to lavish money on her. She continued to expect luxuries, and her parents had bought all the furnishings in his house with the exception of his study furniture and the grandfather clock in the hall that he had bought as a student. They had also given her the gold Mercedes she died in. Mercia hadn't needed his money. She had married him for love. She enjoyed the social aspects of being his partner, and he needed her for those since he disliked them himself.

Knowing she was the right wife for a man in his position, he had married her. Money was the key to happiness. Society respected a wife who knew how much to spend without causing needless envy among her peers. Mercia had the knack. In his circle, many men were in the same position, fortunate enough to have wives willing to turn a blind eye to their partner's occasional indiscretions. After a year of marriage, Hagen knew the rules.

If anyone could have been Mercia's contrast, good-as-gold Marigold was. Although he ragged her about old money, from the moment he had met her he had recognized her innate class. Her family had dropped off the wealthy list a few generations back, but still remained socially significant, mainly on her mother's side. Her father ran a law firm, like his illustrious ancestor, but there the comparison ended. He, like his father before him, thought the world owed him a living. The world didn't agree, and Julian Reynolds had invested his ego in his sons, while ignoring his brave and studious daughter.

Marigold managed because of her strength of character. He had never had more than a few blindsiding kisses from her although he had always wanted more. Unfortunately, that same strength of character kept her out of Hagen's reach. And now he had her back there. What he planned to do about that, he didn't know.

But what he did know was that he no longer needed a memorial to Mercia. The time had come to make his house his own.

* * * *

Wishing she had changed out of her jeans and sweater into something a little smarter, though that would have been too obvious, Marigold tramped up the street toward Hagen's house. The moment she had read his address, she knew exactly where he lived. About four years ago, she had watched with special interest while the workers renovated the old mansion. The fact that he owned the house built by her ancestors on her father's side filled her with a kind of twisted pleasure because at last she would have a chance to take a glimpse of the inside.

She walked the length of the brushwood fence that hid the tennis court and swimming pool from the view of the street. The two-story sandstone mansion had been authentically restored outside to a high standard. Past generations had removed the cast iron moldings but now they sat back in their rightful place, under the eaves and around the veranda. The old black cast iron fence had been repaired and refinished. The place practically glowed.

She swung open the tall front gate and strode down a slate path lined by clipped box hedges that suited the 1870 style of the house, though she doubted the original settlers would have had anything quite so formal outside. A white marble-tiled veranda ran along the front of the house and around the left side. She stepped up, impressed by the restoration. About to lift the knocker on the heavy front door, she heard footsteps, and waited. Sure enough, the door swung open. Hagen still wore his jeans, and he was still heart-stoppingly handsome.

"Exactly on time," he said in a satisfied voice, and he stood aside to let her in the house ahead of him.

"Do you know that my family built this house?" She stared at the whitest hall she had ever seen in her life, the walls, the ceiling, the hall table, and a crazy big chandelier that used roses as candleholders.

"Yes. Come through to the kitchen."

He preceded her past a closed door on either side of the wide hallway, which she knew used to double as the ballroom, heading for the beautiful staircase that had also been painted white, even the thick curved mahogany rail. Her eyes prickled with horror. After a right turn past an old grandfather clock, he headed down another white passageway decorated with a couple of modern paintings. She reached the kitchen, a space blindingly white, very beautiful, but strangely impersonal.

"I watched a lot of the renovation from the outside while passing, but I had no idea you owned the house," she said, standing by the island countertop. "Though now I look at the front garden, I can see Calli designed it. I think my ancestors would have been thrilled to bits to have one so gracious. Those old palms that used to be here were ghastly." She shifted her bag to her other shoulder.

"I had some qualms about removing them, but Calli assured me that they would keep growing and dropping fronds for another few hundred years if I didn't. Since they were badly out of place from the start, I decided I could dispense with them. We're eating in the breakfast room."

"Breakfast room?" She stared at the doorway she assumed led to the garage. "I haven't heard anyone say 'breakfast room' since Grandfather Grace."

"According to the old records of the house, the room was called the breakfast room and the breakfast room it shall remain." He indicated the way.

She stepped though the doorway that led to two more doorways, one of which was open and let in a blare of sunlight. The other would be the inside entry to the garage. In the center of the small table, she spotted enough sandwiches to keep a group of gossiping biddies silent for an hour or two. She decided to ignore the fact that this room was white as well because of the late spring sunshine peeping though the bank of windows and the view of the sparkling new green growth in the garden. "I'll have to be careful not to drop a slice of tomato in here."

He sighed. "I know the room is white. I heard you not mention the fact."

"There's no doubt that I'm mistress of the obvious. The room is beautiful, nonetheless." She offered a placating smile.

He indicated the small plate in front of her and the platter of sandwiches. "Help yourself."

She took the nearest grouping, a variety of various meats and salads and placed them on her sandwich plate. "I presume we make small talk until we've eaten and then we'll get down to business."

"I can't see the harm in us being civil to each other for a while. It's been a long time coming."

She lifted her head and stared at him. "I'm not assuming you bought my family's house to show me up, you know."

"I bought it because it's beautiful and I like this area."

"You're not too far from where your parents live. Well, approximately. Kensington and St. Peters are on the same side of the city."

He shrugged. "And if I'd had children, I could send them to our old school."

"That's why my mother wanted me there, that and because it's her old school, too. Having a school within walking distance is a treat."

"Though a slight disadvantage. I know your mother had to put up with my sisters after school, or at any odd time."

"She loved them. She would have had more children if she could, but it's not done when you don't have a husband."

"You mean 'not done,'" he said, making air quotes.

"Yes. I know it's done, but it was not done in my mother's circles."

"Or yours."

"Having been brought up by a single parent, I wouldn't do the same to my child. I would want my children to have a loving father."

He looked away, taking up a sandwich and biting into the bread as if he needed to dispose of the distraction and get on with showing her his house.

She took the hint and ate as fast as she could, while deciding not to offer small talk in case she sprayed crumbs. Instead she gazed at the garden, realizing that the silence was companionable rather than fraught. Before he offered her one of the many sweet treats sitting in the kitchen, she said, "What is the budget for the dinner?"

He shrugged. "Whatever I would pay to take this lot out to an expensive restaurant."

"Although I don't want the fact widely known, I've rarely been to the sort of expensive restaurant you mean. Give me a figure to work with."

"Let's say two hundred a head."

"Including wine?"

He shook his head. "Far has a good cellar. As soon as the menu is set, send it to him, and he'll make a match for the courses. He sees selecting the perfect wines for food as a hobby."

"Does your father need a hobby when he works a hundred hours a week?"

"Everyone needs a hobby no matter how many hours he or she works. Surely you have one?"

"Some might say my work is my hobby," she answered with an amount of self-derision. "I certainly earn money at hobby rates. Now, let me see your sitting and dining rooms."

He arose slowly, as if he would rather stay and eat but she couldn't sit with him for hours. She had lost her head over him a long time ago, and she wanted to take it back. Being cozy with him didn't help in the least.

"This way." He led her through the kitchen and along the marble-tiled passage, opening the first door into a white dining room. Her initial thought was to say, *What a surprise,* but sarcasm didn't suit the moment. Instead she said, "White is an easy color to work with. That table extends to fit ten?"

"It has various sized leaves. I believe I can seat twenty, but I never have."

"So, onward to the sitting room."

The extra door in the dining room opened in front of the stairway into the vast empty space of the main hall. Directly across, the main sitting room still featured the original white marble fireplace. Atop sat an empty white vase. The only color relief other than the pale gray fitted carpet was the view of the side garden through the glass of the French windows. White leather modern seating had been artfully arranged around the room. Glass side tables stood cold and empty.

"Do you mind if I change each of the rooms a little, to make them a little more cozy for your guests? In here perhaps a colorful rug on the floor and a few cushions. They would be borrowed from the warehouse."

"I don't mind what you do. You are the set designer of this show."

"And I need to inspect your plates and your silverware, too." She almost winced at the intrusion into his solitary life.

"You won't be surprised to find that the plates are white, will you?"

"Not surprised, no."

"Nor pleased."

"I can work with white in the dining room. It's easy enough to add color with the table dressings."

He stood, staring at her. "The chimneys are unblocked in the sitting and dining rooms. I could arrange for a log fire on the night."

"That would be wonderful, Hagen, not only for the chill factor but also because people tend to relax around fires."

"I wouldn't know. We didn't want smoke to stain the walls." He turned his face away.

She wanted to hug him. This must be so difficult, seeing his house with a stranger's eyes. Likely everything she did or said reminded him that Mercia had gone. Instead, she reached out a hand and gripped his for a moment. "We won't stain her walls. I'll personally clean off any smoke damage." Her voice sounded husky.

He squeezed her fingers and drew a breath. "It's been a year, Marigold. I think a few changes are in order." He looked as if he wanted to say something else, but instead he brought the back of her hand to his mouth. The shock of him kissing her hand made her gasp. She quickly pulled away from him. "I must go," she said hurriedly. "I'll collect my bag first. I won't take Monday off. I enjoy working away from home."

She practically ran to get her bag from the breakfast room, as awkward as she had been at sixteen.

"I'm sorry," he said at the front door. "My manners are all over the place these days and that was inappropriate. It was simply…" He shrugged. "Memories."

She nodded because she understood. When anyone reminded her of her mother, she also had sad, lost feelings. "I know, Hagen. It won't help if I cry for you. I've cried too much for me, and I know it doesn't make anything better. But I do understand."

She walked home at such a rapid pace, and so lost in her thoughts that she noted nothing until she reached her own shabby front door. She stepped inside her very ordinary house determined not to let her feelings for Hagen overcome her. If he married again, he would choose another Mercia, and Marigold would never be a Mercia. She would never have a spotless white house and an interest in being swamped by celebrities or dressing in wickedly expensive clothes.

If she had paid full price for the dress she had bought today, she would have suffered from a weeklong guilt attack. Then again, for years she had barely spent a cent that wasn't calling out to be spent on something useful. Maybe after three months earning a salary, she could be more casual about money, not as casual as Hagen, but more relaxed. At least she would have an amount to spend.

She had an idea when Hagen had mentioned his father's interest in wine. Knowing his mother was equally interested in food, and having heard Demi Allbrook used to manage the business dinners before Mercia had taken over, she picked up the landline and dialed the number she had often dialed before, looking for either Calli or Tiggy—Demi Allbrook's number. These days she probably used a smart phone but Marigold didn't have her number.

The phone rang three times, and, "Hello," said Demi's voice.

Marigold spent the breath she had been holding. "Hi, Demi. It's Marigold Reynolds here. I want to talk business, but I'll call back on a weekday if you would prefer to relax without business intruding into your life on a Saturday afternoon."

"Marigold!" Demi said with a clear exclamation mark. She tended to use many in her speech. "Darling! You can talk to me about anything you like. I've been meaning to drop into your office to welcome you, but I thought I'd give you a minute or two to settle in. How are you managing?"

"I'm not Tiggy, by any means. The best I can say is that I'm trying. I've just had lunch with Hagen—"

"Hagen! Oh, dear Lord, Alex!" she said raising her voice. Marigold could imagine Alex Allbrook's glance of polite interest at his wife. "Marigold had lunch with Hagen. He says he's impressed, Marigold. None of us have had anything other than a business meal with him for the past year."

"I don't want to burst your bubble, Demi, but it was a business lunch. I had a look at his house so that I would know what I'm working with for this dinner of his. He told me the budget, and I'm supposed to find a caterer. It's all so last minute and I don't think it will be easy. I was hoping, since you have done this sort of thing before, if you have any recommendations?"

For a moment, she heard nothing but silence and she worried that somehow she had stepped out of line. "Didn't Tiggy book anyone?" Demi sounded puzzled.

"If so, I can't find an annotation. It only says in her notes to organize Hagen's dinner. I presumed it was to organize the table decorations or the place cards in a restaurant. Instead, I need to do the whole thing in his house from whoa to go."

"I have a few ideas," Demi said in a slow and thoughtful voice. "Let me get back to you tomorrow. A celebrity chef wouldn't be available on short notice and you wouldn't want one anyway. You want a good cook who is content to stay in the background. What fun! I'll call you back as soon as I have some choices for you. Bye, darling Marigold."

Marigold sat for a while, half stunned, and grinning like a fool. At best, she'd imagined Demi would suggest a few names. Instead, the adorable woman would give her hands-on help. Even if Marigold's mother had still been alive, she couldn't have given Marigold any catering advice. Her kidney failure made her social life almost non-existent and the idea of knowing a celebrity chef would have caused her to smile with puzzlement. She knew doctors and lawyers, but no Indian chiefs, or chefs as the case might have been.

Marigold breathed out with satisfaction. One step almost completed. If the food was organized, she could manage the rest. Her mother had made sure that Marigold knew from an early age the niceties of table settings, introductions, protocols, precedence, and all those other old-fashioned courtesies that had almost been lost these days. Even for breakfast, Marigold had flowers on the table in her own house. For her, flower arranging was habit. She could only guess but from the look of Mercia's white table, the decorations she used would have been expensive and not acquainted with either soil or water.

Now for her next step. Having seen Hagen's dining room and the way all the character had been painted out of his house, she'd had an idea about the setting she could use for his guests. Visitors to a house as old as his would be interested in the history. Being related to the original builder meant she knew this. She didn't plan to spout off about her family, but she could offer the house some original color.

To this end, she reapplied her lipstick, changed her top into a polo neck, added a jacket, and strode outside to her car, deliberately not calling first to see if her father might be at home. Her stepmother usually answered the phone and managed not to be able to find him. Marigold didn't assume this was Jane, her stepmother's choice, but her father's decision not to speak to his daughter, who could admit to a fairly adversarial relationship with her only living parent.

Fortunately, he lived close in a modern house in Burnside. Her half brothers had been brought up in comfortable circumstances and appeared to see her as an intrusion, which galled Marigold. And she was tired of never confronting the various issues she had had with being treated that way.

She pulled up her car in his driveway, and strode to the front entrance. The buzz of the bell called Jane to the door with a surprised smile.

"Have I caught Julian at home?"

"He's watching the football on TV with the boys. Come in, Marigold." Jane was a small neat woman with brown eyes and dark curly hair. She wore colors that didn't suit her, autumn colors, which meant that she looked sallow, a shame because she had an outgoing disposition, unlike Julian, Marigold's father. She wished she could say she liked her father, but mainly she felt sorry for him; he had missed every opportunity his daughter gave him to love and respect him.

He barely turned his head as Jane announced Marigold's arrival. "Sit down."

She sat. "I'm not here to watch football on television. I want to borrow the Royal Doulton dinner setting."

He finally glanced at her. "My grandmother's set?"

"Yes. It should be mine. She handed it down to your mother, and Grandma Reynolds said you were keeping it for me." She raised her chin.

"That's the first time I've heard that," Jane said in a fussed voice. "It's quite valuable. I thought we would divide it up for the boys. It's certainly big enough."

"I didn't ask to keep it. I asked to borrow it." Marigold smiled firmly. Her father frowned. "Do you want it?"

"I asked for it, didn't I?"

"Give it to her, Jane. I don't see the point of dividing it up for the boys. They might marry women who can't stand old things. I can't myself."

"Give it to me?"

"If my mother meant it for you, you can have it." He glanced at the TV as if it might disappear if he didn't concentrate.

Her brothers, eighteen and sixteen, glanced at her as if she were crazy. "Plates," Jamie said. "I don't want plates. Do you want plates, Joff?"

"Nope. Hi, Marigold."

"Hi, Joff and James. I won't disturb your TV watching any longer. Can I take the plates now?"

"I'll need a while to pack them." Jane moistened her lips. "I've got them in the storeroom. One of the boys will take them to your house tomorrow. What do you want them for?"

"A dinner. But I really want them because they were meant to be mine. If I thought you used them, it would be a different matter, but I know you don't. I know most people wouldn't, but I would. I love the set. I used to help Grandma wash it after we had eaten. Thank you, Julian. I'll be on my way now."

Her father didn't stand, he didn't walk her to the door, and he didn't say good-bye. He watched TV and left Jane to see her out.

Chapter 4

Marigold washed the whole Royal Doulton set right after the box arrived via her brother Jamie on his way to football practice on Sunday morning. The aqua-blue and white setting had been edged with a lacy gold pattern, and she placed each elegantly simple piece on her dining room table, plotting her setting for Hagen's dinner.

Although using a plain white arrangement of flowers as the centerpiece would set off the colorful runner she had decided the table needed, she had in mind using a gold-etched treasure, one that had belonged to her mother's family. She removed the bowl from the china cabinet, placing the fine porcelain in the center of her mother's old mahogany table. Standing back to admire the effect, she realized that she hadn't used the dining room in a year. On her own now, she normally ate at the small table in the kitchen, a habit she decided to break. She loved pretty things, and she had deprived herself for no real reason.

Now was perhaps the time to make grown-up decisions about the way she lived. She still occupied her childhood bedroom. After her mother's death, she had packed up everything and returned the hospital bed, the wheelchair, and the bathroom safety bars. Knowing reminders would make her weep, Marigold hadn't been in her mother's room since, except to stand and stare.

She opened the door to the main bedroom in the house, marched across the bare floorboards, and jerked open the curtains. Light flooded into the musty, empty space. Blinking resolutely, she pulled out the boxes she had left stored in the cupboards and checked the labels. Clothes: time to offer each neatly folded garment to the charity shop. Old letters and cards, jewelry box, mementos: keep. Stationary, tax returns, dried up pens, a broken watch: no use to anyone.

She took the clothes out to the garage to drop off tomorrow. With some reluctance, she threw out the sentimental keeps no one would ever use, watching each piece drop to the bottom of the bin, her heart aching. However, the memories she had kept inside her would always be more long-lasting than mementos. Now with the bedroom almost empty, she placed her mother's treasures with her own. That done, she cleaned the bedroom from top to bottom, revealing a shabby paint job and a beautiful wooden floor.

Contemplating the room with her hands on her hips, she decided on the placement of her bedroom furniture into the larger space. But first she would paint the room in one of the colors of the patchwork quilt her mother had made. She chose the dark blue.

Nothing would please her more than being able to renovate the whole house, but even with a three-month salary she wouldn't be able to afford to do much more than change a few colors. Nevertheless, as a property stylist, she should certainly have done far more in the time since her mother's death. Apathy had overcome her, but having a real job had moved her head into new space.

* * * *

On Monday at work, she sorted out the furnishings she might use to showcase the duplex school building, though Hagen's dinner mainly occupied her mind. After lunch when he returned from whatever meeting he'd been attending, she said to him, "At some time, I'll need to polish your silver and get your table napkins starched."

"Why does that sound suggestive?" He placed his hand on his door, too handsome and too perfectly groomed for her peace of mind.

She raised her eyebrows. "Because you've apparently been to an all guy's meeting," she answered in a voice of forced patience. "And you've probably been innuendo-ing each other to death."

"Hm. Not a bad guess. Don't worry about the silver or the napkins. I'll get my daily to attend to those. I hope that doesn't sound suggestive."

"Nope." She turned and saw Sandra's eyebrows on the way down.

Hagen shut his office door and Sandra muttered, "It sounds like he's back in the land of the living."

"It does? Has he always been a lecher?" Marigold asked with a straight face.

Sandra laughed. "For a while there, he wouldn't have recognized an innuendo if it whacked him in the face. His male hormones are returning."

"Good to hear," Marigold said, marching into her own office, unsettled. If Hagen were about to turn into a rampant male, she would be in danger, not of being accosted, but of wilting from envy when he chose his next woman. She picked up her black pen and tapped her chin before beginning on a sketch of the outside of Hagen's house. Picturing the angle of the roof, she had her concentration interrupted by a phone call. Demi Allbrook.

"Hi, Demi. Do you have good news for me?"

"Sure do. A lovely young chef, who is currently working with Rob Megnam at Eight's Late, will cater your dinner. Rob doesn't think it will do his business any harm to have his best apprentice cooking a meal for the high end of town."

"You are a wonderful woman, Demi. So, I should meet with him to discuss the menu."

"Exactly what I thought. I made a booking for lunch tomorrow for you and me at Eight's Late. That'll be a business lunch. Tell that to your boss." Demi sounded satisfied.

Marigold laughed. "My boss spends so much time himself out of the office that he won't notice if I leave. It will be good to have the food off my plate, so to speak. What time shall we meet?"

"I'll pick you up at midday. Bye, darling!"

Marigold finished off the house sketch, and scanned the black-and-white picture into the computer. The next quarter hour she spent online designing a white business-size card with her shrunken drawing placed in a line along the top. She ordered fifty from the site. Then she found a use for Tiggy's scalpel by cutting out a half A2-size stencil of the house.

With the whole table setting now organized she put her mind to the rest of Hagen's sitting room. In the warehouse, she found a large floor rug in jewel colors. This would cover part of the marble tiles in the hall. Another she found in similar colors could be placed in the sitting room. She dusted off her hands, knowing she could find the right cushions to add warmth to the white leather seating. Tonight at home she would make the silk table runner she had decided on for his dining table. As far as she was concerned, the dinner was done.

The next morning, she dressed carefully, wanting to look suitably businesslike to the chef who would be preparing Hagen's dinner. Through the glass panels in her office door, she saw Demi arrive at midday. Demi veered into Hagen's office first. She came out with a satisfied smile.

"Ready?" she said to Marigold who stood waiting, her bag hitched over her shoulder.

"You look gorgeous," Marigold said, her smile wide.

Demi was a good-looking woman of medium height and in her middle fifties. She wore a cream suit with a striped silk blouse. Her bag and shoes were tan, smart, and expensive, and her dark hair was blunt cut just below her ears. "I don't have as many chances to go out to lunch with a young person as I would like, and you look lovely yourself, Marigold. You always know the perfect colors to wear."

Marigold had few choices. For work, she owned a black jacket, a black skirt, and black pants. Other than that, she had a few different tops. Today she wore a black-and-white striped blouse, which played off the light red-gold of her hair. She kissed Demi on the cheek, and Demi tucked her hand under Marigold's arm and led her outside to the car, a silver Beamer.

As soon as she had pulled out onto the road, Demi said, "It's good of you to take over from Tiggy at a moment's notice. She couldn't have left if she didn't know she had someone she could trust to do her work."

"She's got a mean old boss," Marigold said, smiling mischievously. "I know he would have made it very difficult for her to get time off without an instant replacement."

Demi glanced at her. "Which one? Alex or Hagen?"

"I was thinking of Alex. I was always so sorry for her, being stuck with a father who gave her everything her devious little heart desired and also helped her with her homework."

"We all have our cross to bear," Demi said, laughing. "I'm glad you're getting on with Hagen. You two were always good together. He's not so easy to deal with these days."

Marigold had no intention of talking about Hagen or his moods. "He's the invisible man. That's the best sort of boss to have when you don't have any idea how to do a job you've been told you will find easy. By the time I think I know some of the answers, Tiggy will be back. She was quite mysterious about what she is doing. Is she being overly modest about her volunteering work?"

"I'm sure she's not."

"What is she doing in Cambodia?" Marigold asked directly.

"I'm sure she'll tell you when she arrives back. Now, should I be doing a righthand turn here?"

"The next crossing. The more I don't know what's going on with her, the curiouser and curiouser I get."

"It's a common failing, my darling. I'll turn just up here, then."

Marigold sighed. Demi would give her nothing, and Marigold couldn't understand why. "You can trust me."

"I know, darling, I know, but I can't tell another's secret, now can I?"

"You told me I was like a daughter to you," Marigold said in her grumbling voice. "Okay. I won't ask again."

"Thank you." Demi briefly rested her hand on Marigold's knee and then she negotiated her way through the narrow street on the outskirts of the city where Eight's Late was sited. "Rob said I could park out the front of the restaurant. That's if anyone left a space."

Marigold gave an amused glance. "I can already see the perfect space, not quite in front, but one all the same."

"We're early." Demi looked satisfied. "The crowds won't arrive for another hour. I'm not so much lucky as crafty. I don't like trying to find parks around here." She pulled up in an angled park and swung out of the car.

Marigold did the same and met Demi on the footpath. "Lead on."

The warm and cozy restaurant was furnished with wood tables, black leather chairs, and a dark patterned carpet. The waiter led them to a table for two, set with water and glasses and white starched napkins. "The balsamic chicken here is divine," Demi said as she scanned the menu. "I've had it before. But you'll need to save yourself for dessert."

"Good idea. I never bother with dessert at home. I think I have to try lamb shanks in red wine."

"Your family used to own Hagen's house, didn't they?" Demi leaned back after they had ordered.

"Long story in a nutshell. My great-grandfather inherited a fortune and the house from his father, who was one of the first settlers. He did well. He was the only son and a lawyer, too, but his son—my grandfather—helped his two brothers lose or spend most of their inheritance. None of them could afford the upkeep on the family home, and so the property was sold."

"After three generations. How sad."

"That's the problem when there's no primogeniture. My father had three siblings, so he inherited nothing but a quarter of his father's property, which wasn't much anyway. Luckily he married my mother who had her parents' tiny new house."

"And that's where you live now."

"Haven't moved an inch. I'm just about to do the place up. I thought a lick of paint here and there would make the world of difference."

"Would you do it yourself?"

"Uh, huh. I don't have a problem with the physical aspects of designing, that is, making things look good. The problem I have is in the business side. I'm not used to making endless phone calls to track down how to do the job I'm expected to do."

"That sounds very frustrating, but what do you need to track down? Didn't Tiggy leave you instructions?"

"She probably thought I would know more than I do know. For instance, I have a note in her book for today that says, 'Do the reception area for Rundle Street.' What reception area, where on Rundle Street, and do what to the reception area? Sandra gave me the lowdown on the Rundle Street property, but she doesn't know what I should do or when."

Demi tucked a lock of her hair behind her ear. "Ask Hagen."

"These questions are so piddling, Demi. I can't interrupt him every half hour. Aside from that, most times I don't know where he is."

"Give me your phone."

Marigold fossicked in her bag and passed over her phone.

"This is an antique," Demi said with a frown. "We must get you a better one. You should have a company phone. In the meantime, I'll put in Hagen's number." Demi fiddled for a while and then she showed Marigold what she had done. "Call him if you can't find him."

"He has important things to do, and I shouldn't interrupt."

"When he can't be interrupted, he will turn off his phone."

Marigold stared. "Are you sure he won't yell at me?"

"No." Demi smiled carefully. "You will cope if he does, though. You could always get him out of a mood. We all used to love the way you distracted him."

"You all?"

"As a lad, he was always too serious for his own good. He was very conscious of being the older brother and he thought he had to look after his sisters. He included you in that group, too, and it was so funny the way you wouldn't let him. He never quite knew what to do with you."

Marigold wrinkled her nose. "I'm an only child. I wasn't used to reacting in a family group. I expected to be independent."

"I know it's tough without your mother, sweetheart, but we're here for you." Demi reached out and covered Marigold's hand. A presence loomed behind her, and she glanced up with a smile. "Food already? Thank you," she said to the waitress. She gave one last squeeze of Marigold's hand.

Marigold breathed in the aroma of the rosemary and bay leaf. The lamb dish had been slow cooked and the first tender mouthful slid down her throat, leaving behind the taste of the rich red-wine sauce. "This is gorgeous. Thank you for bringing me to this place." Again, she mulled over Demi's word *all*. The whole family had watched Hagen's reaction to her? She wished she had watched it herself. She had no idea she distracted Hagen, and she gave a little wriggle of pleasure.

"Hagen needs distraction these days," Demi said, as if channeling Marigold's thoughts. She cut off another slice of her herbed chicken. "It's not for me to say how long a person should mourn, but he hasn't taken a day off work since Mercia died, and I know he doesn't have a social life. It wouldn't hurt him to laugh once in a while. You could always make him relax."

"Perhaps he feels too guilty to laugh. When my mother died, I did. I kept thinking I should have spent every waking minute with her because I always knew she would die soon, but not when. And sometimes I went out with friends."

"But you know you shouldn't feel guilty about that."

"I do. But it's worse for Hagen. He had such a short time with Mercia. I was not surprised when I heard he was going to marry her." Marigold swallowed awkwardly. "She was kind of perfect for him."

"At first, I couldn't see what they had in common, but she certainly knew how to play the role of the corporate wife. She dressed beautifully, and she was the perfect hostess."

"I don't suppose anyone will ever match her," Marigold said in a gruff voice. Of course Hagen had chosen the perfect wife. That's what golden men did.

"I don't suppose anyone will." Demi concentrated on her plate for a moment and then said, "What do you think about the plans for the new tramline the government wants to give us?"

Marigold had an opinion but perfect Mercia remained in the back of her mind until the last plate was removed and a stocky dark-eyed young man, her age or a little more, pulled a chair over to their table. "I'm Sam Habib, Rob's assistant chef."

Demi shook his hand, Marigold shook his hand, and he sat, his portfolio on his lap. "I have three menus here for you to look at. I'll want to know which you prefer by Thursday."

"I think Marigold can make up her mind right now," Demi said firmly.

Marigold scanned the menus. "The dinner is for men and women, so we'll want the lighter meat dish for mains. Rum beef ribs, perhaps? What do you think about a fish entrée, Demi? Or should we have something vegetarian?"

"Prawns and fennel. That looks nice."

"Yes. I suppose we don't want to bloat everyone before dessert." Marigold grinned at Sam who returned her smile cautiously.

"Will you want a cheese platter, too?" he asked, holding her gaze.

"Fruit and cheese. And canapés to welcome the guests. Truffles."

"Truffles?"

"I don't think I'm spending enough money," Marigold said with mock guilt. "Hagen said about two hundred dollars per head."

Demi stared at Marigold. "Perhaps that's how Mercia did it, but it's not compulsory to spend that much. If a menu works for you, that's what you should have. Right, Sam?"

"My boss wouldn't mind if she wants to spend a fortune," Sam answered, smiling at Marigold. He was a good-looking, broad-shouldered man with eyelashes as dark as the stubble on his buzz cut.

"I think as long as we can pass around vegetable dishes and salads—and perhaps include a substitute meal for anyone who has a problem with the table menu—that we will be okay."

Demi breathed out. "You don't want to start listening to Hagen's catering ideas."

"I took them with a grain of salt, Demi. Trust me." Marigold turned to Sam. "On the night, we will be using an antique dinner set that can't be put in the dishwasher. You will make sure your server washes every piece by hand, won't you?"

Sam aimed a careful glance at her. "The waitress who is serving you today is the one Rob asked to help. She is efficient with service and responsible enough to look after the customer's property."

"I'll have a word with her before we leave, then. Okay, no truffles, but you will do a good selection of canapés, won't you?"

"I have your e-mail address. I'll send you a mock up tomorrow of everything I will prepare." Sam rose to his feet, clutching his notes, and left. His back view was kind of manly, too. While Marigold mulled that, she realized that she also was having a return of hormones. She thought Hagen was the only man she could look at and appreciate, but apparently she could also enjoy other men.

Congratulating herself on the return of her good sense, she left with Demi and was dropped at the huge front doors of the AA & Co. multistory building. Normally she used the back entrance. Like a successful negotiator, she strode through the glass-roofed atrium to her office, where Hagen stood at Sandra's desk apparently waiting for a printout. He glanced up at Marigold. "So, you've taken to business lunches as to the manor born."

"Now I know what I've been missing all these years," she answered flippantly.

"You don't want my mother leading you astray."

She straightened. "Of course I do. I've been waiting to be led astray for many years and this is my first chance. Do you want to hear all this, Sandra?"

Sandra folded her arms and leaned back. "I wouldn't miss it for the world."

"I meant," he said frowning, "that you don't have to take her advice."

"I appreciate her advice."

"You don't need to be polite about her. I know she likes to meddle, and I know she thinks her way is best."

"You're speaking from a son's point of view. I'm speaking from a learner event co-coordinator's point of view. If I didn't have her help, I would be floundering."

He spread his hands and stared at her, clearly not about to offer his help. Frustrated, she huffed back into her office.

* * * *

Hagen didn't want to work with Marigold. He didn't want to be near her day after day. He didn't want to laugh when she laughed, and he didn't want her to get on with his mother. Mercia hadn't. She had disliked Demi and said she was a control freak. He could have cut the atmosphere between the two of them with a knife and a man had to be loyal to his wife, even if he couldn't see that his mother had too many faults. Naturally, as Mercia said, he was biased.

When he sighed, Sandra said, "You have to admit that since Marigold has been here, you've had a load of meetings. I can't help her with Tiggy's job. I'm nothing more than a glorified typist."

"Who says you're glorified?" He folded his arms.

She smiled. "I haven't been insulted by you for a year. Welcome back."

With no idea what she was talking about, he stalked into his office, glad that he had found so much to do that he had a perfect excuse not to be at Marigold's beck and call. If he were available most of the time, she would be bothering him with questions, or asking him if he wanted to have coffee with her in the staff room, or she might touch him or smile at him. Since Saturday at his house when he had grabbed her hand like a pathetic sex-starved widower, he had known he couldn't trust himself with her. If she hadn't dragged her hand away, he might have snatched her into his arms, thrown her across his shoulders, and raced her up the stairs to his bedroom.

Mercia's bedroom.

He breathed out. Fortunately, during the dinner at his house, business associates would surround him and serve as chaperones. His lust for the redhead would remain unsatisfied. When she had been suggested for Tiggy's job, he had been dead against the idea, but with both his parents and his sisters on the other side, his vote didn't count. He sat staring at the wall until his office door swung open and Marigold stood staring at him.

She hitched up her lovely mouth and gave an apologetic smile. "Hagen, I'm sorry I was rude to you about your mother. I'm a bit sensitive about mothers these days, the same way you're sensitive about wives. Let's not be mean to each other."

He concentrated on her worried tawny eyes and her expression of helplessness. "Let's not." He stared at her until she turned and walked out again. He would have to grow immune to her presence, and he would have to grow used to the fact that when she laughed, he laughed.

* * * *

Marigold arrived at Hagen's house at six on Friday night, dressed for what she considered to be her role, that of an event co-coordinator. She had wavered over her gray-and-black dress after she had spent the morning adding color to his house, and she had decided not to add color to herself. Dressing discreetly would make her seem more like part of the service team than a guest. She had plaited a knot of hair on the nape of her neck and as a touch of femininity she wore her mother's pearl-drop earrings.

When he answered the door to her, Hagen scanned her from head to toe. He had always known how to dress, and his camel-colored trousers and a black knit clung to his broad shoulders and showed off his flat belly. His eyebrows lifted. "You look very nice."

"I hope I look like a background noise," she answered ruefully.

"You are a beautiful woman, Marigold. You will always stand out in a crowd. You owe it to other women to occasionally wear something that they can compete with instead of simply your coloring and your elegant bones."

She gave an impatient click of her tongue. "You still judge people by the price of their clothes. I know you will look good no matter what you wear. I'm quite happy to admire you in anything."

One side of his mouth lifted up. "I will await that happy event."

"So, we lied to each other." Remaining cool, she shrugged. "You told me I was beautiful, and I told you that you were admirable."

He looked down at her. "You lied. I told the truth for a change. You are incredibly beautiful. I'm sorry I wasn't home while you were turning my house on end but without my supervision you have done a superlative job. Thank you." Indicating she should come inside, he stood back and waited.

Incredibly beautiful? Willing herself to believe that the man who had once called her scrawny thought so. Shivering with the thrill of the compliment, she entered and after he had closed the door, she followed him across the colorful carpet she had placed in the hallway. Enjoying the red vase full of arum lilies she had arranged on the white hall table, she focused on his impossibly gorgeous back view. The man had the sort of tight behind that any woman would want to check out with both hands. Her breath hitched. Every tiny cell in her body wanted Hagen—always had—even before the first time he had kissed her.

Fortunately, she turned into the passageway that led to the kitchen and distracted herself by breathing in the herbal aroma of cooking food. "All underway?" she said to Sam as she nodded to Rosie, his helper for the night.

Sam's gaze met hers. "I think we have this under control. Could you check the table setting?"

Rosie wiped the cooking utensils she had finished washing. "I haven't put out the small plates because I wasn't sure which was which. You have so many of different sizes."

"In the old days, they had a plate for every purpose. It will be okay to warm the dishes in the oven, by the way, but not for too long. Just before service, I think. These big flat bowls are for soup. These entrée plates go under the soup dishes. I'll put those and the smaller bread plates on the table. When you remove the soup plates, take the under-plate and the bread plates, too." Marigold gathered up the dishes she had mentioned and took them into the dining room.

Hagen followed. "Where did you find this service?"

"It belonged to my family. I thought that would be an interesting touch to return the plates to the house where they originated."

"They're yours?"

She nodded.

"Antiques? They would be too valuable to use." He frowned.

"I've based the color scheme around them. Plus, if they are never enjoyed, what use are they?"

"This is very generous of you." He sounded stiff.

"Your family has been very generous to me. For many years." She set out the plates and stood back, delighted with the quiet color scheme. The thick aqua silk runner down the center of the table, the white cutouts of Hagen's house inset with aqua menu sheets sitting between each set of knifes and forks, all looked elegant. The bright red camellias in her gold and white flower bowl looked stunning. Mercia's elaborate white chandelier hanging low over the table no longer seemed to be the centerpiece. Now the light was dimmed by the tasteful setting. "I don't think it's overdone. I hope you approve."

He picked his own place card and examined the house print on the top. "Where did you find the sketch for this?"

"I drew it." She glanced at him.

He blinked and nodded. "Thank you. Have you taste-tested the canapés?"

"I trust Sam."

"Let me pour you a pre-dinner drink."

"Thank you. Is the fire stoked?"

"I started it when I arrived home. The room is now cozy. We can sit in there awaiting our guests unless you have something vital to attend to now."

"I thought it might be a good idea if you went through the guest list with me. I have learned who is who by name and job, but I would like to know in what way these people can be useful to you."

"Right. I have champagne cooling in the sitting room." He hooked an arm behind her and guided her through the door to the hallway again, and then into the sitting room where the fire crackled cheerfully.

The room looked far more comfortable now. A carpet square brightly patterned in blue, red, and gray sat in front of the fireplace and cushions in the same colors warmed up the sofa and chairs. Again, she had added red camellias on the mantelpiece and a glass side table where the champagne cooler sat with fine-etched glasses. He poured out two measures and she sat on the couch with him in order to study the guest list.

Chapter 5

Hagen's parents arrived first. Each kissed Marigold. His mother, dressed in a white silk shirt with a blue silk skirt, admired the room and seemed delighted to see the fire. "So cozy, darling," she said to Marigold who gave a pleased little lift of her shoulders. "You told me you don't have any ideas. That's a wonderful idea. It makes a home out of a house."

Hagen rubbed the back of his neck. "It could be the company rather than the fire," he said, trying not to sound as if he needed to defend Mercia's choices while at the same time realizing that until tonight he had never been particularly comfortable in the sitting room. He poured his parents a drink.

The doorbell rang again and he welcomed the head of the engineering department at the university, Caroline Mason, a brusque shorthaired woman in her fifties who dressed in layers of dusty colored wool. "I've brought along Morgan Evans, my assistant professor," she said in her hearty voice. "I thought he deserved a good meal."

Since Morgan, a chunky, curly haired man in his early thirties, could barely button his tweed jacket, Hagen accepted the statement with a smile and shook each of the pair's hands. Morgan stared at Marigold with a hungry expression on his face. When he held her hand too long, he annoyed the hell out of Hagen. Then the doorbell rang again. Hagen stumped off, disgruntled. If Marigold had been his wife, she could have answered, but he had to leave her with starving Morgan instead.

The politicians had turned up in a group, smartly but casually dressed. One was in government and the other a member of the opposition. While he was ushering them into the sitting room, the government official and his female partner arrived. By this time, Rosie, the waitress, was handing around the canapés.

In due course, after everyone had expressed satisfaction with the champagne, the emu pate, the Stilton and grape bites, and the crab cucumber tartlets, among the other delicacies Marigold had chosen, he ushered everyone into the dining room. He saw the glitch in her seating plan. If she had been his wife...but she wasn't. Therefore, she had put his mother at the other end of the table as the hostess. Instead of sitting near to him, where he wanted her, Marigold had placed herself between the opposition member for planning and infrastructure and Morgan. Hagen had the wife of the member on his right, and the wife of the opposition on his left. Both were diplomatic and determined to enjoy the night out.

However, neither of those ladies was the only woman he could think of lately. He watched Marigold enjoying herself too much, flirting with Morgan and the minister in turn. She had no right to be so at ease in exalted company. She should have been as miserable and bored at this business dinner as Mercia had always been when presented with intellectuals rather than the socially savvy people she ran with.

Instead Marigold was charming all with her natural manner and her offbeat humor. Not only that, but her dinner service was a great hit.

"Where on earth did you find these plates?" The wife of the minister for planning stared at the blue gold-edged setting. "I think these are Royal Doulton but it's not possible. This design hasn't been made for more than a century."

"You'll need to ask Marigold about the plates. She let me borrow them for the night." Hagen took a rather large sip of his red wine.

The woman, Aggie Barwell, made an O of her mouth. "So brave," she said to Marigold. "If we chip these or break one, you will have lost a true treasure."

Mercia would have said, "No matter. We have another twenty," which would show that she could afford to lose a plate or two. Ten years ago, Marigold had told him he was simply a person with someone else's money made from someone else's effort, newly rich, and completely crass.

Remember, most rich families lose their money within the first three generations, she had said, poking one long finger into his chest. *And you're the third.* He had never forgotten that. Her words had preyed on his mind ever since. Although he'd been born with self-confidence, a man had to take into account the fact that he needed to work hard to maintain his family's professional standards.

And as one who knew firsthand what happened to the third generation of money, she now said, "The dishes were meant to be used. It's a shame to keep them for best and never enjoy them yourself, don't you think?"

"I'm honored," Aggie said in her careful voice. Her father had also been a politician and she made the perfect wife for another with her inbuilt charm and tact. "To be eating from something this precious is a first for me. How did you come to own this set?"

"I inherited it, but the reason we are using the set tonight is because it originally belonged to the house. I thought putting the plates and the house together one more time would be rather special."

"I'm honored, too," said Susan Payne, the wife of the other politician. "My parents have some lovely old things they never use and it does seem to be a waste."

This moved the group into reminiscing. Marigold managed to turn the conversation to one of the newer AA projects, which then led to the proposed one, which had been the purpose of the dinner. Hagen no longer had the urge to compare Marigold to Mercia. He had never been more conscious of his greatest mistake, six years ago, assuming he could have Marigold, which rankled tonight more than ever.

Finally, when the last dish had been removed from the table, he ushered the now replete and mellow company back into the sitting room for a glass of his father's treasured old brandy. The fire crackled, his guests settled comfortably, and Rosie appeared in the doorway. She caught Marigold's glance, and the two disappeared. Marigold returned and sidled up to him. "The staff has cleaned up and gone. I told them they were magnificent."

Aggie turned and said, "I should have thanked them, too. The meal was perfectly prepared and presented. I think Doug and I could use Eight's Late for our dinners, too."

"I'll find you a card. I have one in my bag in the kitchen." And Marigold disappeared again.

Not long after she returned, his parents made departure noises, which the rest of the company picked up, leaving Marigold with him. The silence lingered while he stared at her, noting her natural elegance, her beautiful clear skin, her shiny bright hair, and the way she avoided his gaze. Her body language told him he couldn't have her. Once upon a time, he had thought he loved her. Back then, after she had spurned him, he had thought he would never desire another woman.

"Sit," he told her in an impartial voice, using an indifferent smile. "Now is your chance to relax and put up your feet. You and your plates were a great success tonight."

"We probably need to thank your mother for the success. She put me onto Sam and Rosie. The meal was superb and the unobtrusive service was delightful. I won't waste any more of your time, but do you think you could help me carry the dinner service to my car?"

"No," he said promptly. "I wouldn't consider doing any such thing at this time of night. You'll have to get it out again at the other end, and I think that is the least I can do for you. I'll bring it to you tomorrow. Will you be home sometime in the afternoon? I know you shop in the morning." Trying not to show his uncertainty, he plunged his hands into his trouser pockets and stood, his chin raised, staring at her lovely face.

"That would be nice. Yes, I'll be home in the afternoon. Now, brrr."

"Brrr?"

"It's cold outside. I didn't think to bring a jacket. I had too much else on my mind. I'm not exactly longing to brave the night."

"If you're wanting a jacket or a coat, I can give you at least one."

"At least one?" She laughed. "One would be plenty. That would be very chivalrous, and I won't say no."

"Follow me, then." He stepped through the doorway and made his way to the hallway.

"I'm allowed to choose?" She sounded puzzled, but she followed behind him.

"I wouldn't give you any old thing. I have a selection upstairs." He kept his tone casual.

"Lead on." She laughed.

He had to admit to a touch of indecision. Taking the stairs, he continued talking to relax her, or himself. "I have a private boutique of clothes, all brand new and hoping to be worn before they pass into antiquity." He paused at the top landing. Guiding her into his bedroom challenged the past and fought hidden memories. "Step inside." He opened the door into a room whose décor she wouldn't like. He didn't like his white bedroom either, but he hadn't been able to bring himself to make a change while he needed to atone.

"I don't know if I'm comfortable wandering into your bedroom."

"I quite understand." He tried for a remote voice. "I don't like the décor either, but I have a large room through here full of clothes. It's called a dressing room because we like, liked, to be able to say to our friends that we have separate dressing rooms." He opened the door to the area that had once been Mercia's. "I won't crowd you. Go in there and choose whatever you want. All of it, if you like. I would be glad to have the clothes removed but my daily, Imelda, wouldn't hear of it. She took away everything Mercia had worn and donated it to the AIDS Society, but she said that was enough and that the new clothes needed to go elsewhere. I have never discovered an elsewhere."

"Are you telling me that this is a roomful of clothes that have never been worn?"

"The price tags are still intact, as you can see."

She glanced along the row of clothes that Mercia bought and hadn't gotten around to wearing. "I can see at least two coats. How weird. Why would you buy two coats if you didn't need them?"

"For emergencies, I presume," he answered drily, watching a crease form between Marigold's eyebrows.

"I don't want to wear Mercia's clothes." She skimmed a dismissive finger along a line of evening dresses.

"I no longer have any of her clothes. I consider these to be my clothes. Everything here was delivered after she died. Mercia had a plan for my money which she didn't share with me."

She scrutinized his expression. "Oh, damn. This is a Burberry." Her hand lingered on a camel-colored coat. "I can't leave a Burberry to be eaten by moths."

"Take it. Here's a scarf to match the lining. And a bag." He stuffed the scarf into the bag and pulled a cream knit and a dark blue knit from the hangers and shoved them on top, remembering Marigold's comment about a higher wage meaning she could buy a few new things to wear. Until now, he hadn't connected the dots. Of course she couldn't afford the luxuries he had hanging in this room and going to waste. "Please. You will be doing me a favor." He slid the coat off the rack and held it open for Marigold to don.

With a wary glance at him, she slipped her hands through the sleeves. In the circle of his outstretched arms, he wrapped her into the fine wool, wishing he could hold her close against his heart and rest his face in her warm glossy hair.

She moved away closing two buttons. "She and I are the same size," she said, her palm flat on her belly as she glanced at herself in the mirrored wall at the back of the room.

"You're taller but the coat is still a good fit. Now, although I would love to entertain you in my bedroom all night, I think for the sake of my sanity we should grab these things and leave."

She gave him a sideways, quizzical glance. "Are you finding being in a bedroom together unnerving?"

"Somewhat." He twisted his mouth into the semblance of a smile. "And, unfortunately, too intimate."

She nodded. "Let's not be awkward about this. I know you well enough to feel perfectly safe with you. As for the coat, as gorgeous as it is, I'm not sure I should take it." She smoothed the fabric over her slim hips while she lingered over her decision.

"Please. Even I can see these clothes are well worth the money spent and I would like someone worthy to have them, someone who will do justice to the price." Which Mercia had never done. For her, shopping was a competitive sport. She wanted the best and the most expensive and she thought being complimented for the way she dressed was meaningful. Marigold, on the other hand, took compliments as polite encouragement, which for most people they were.

"I don't want to disregard Mercia's memory," Marigold answered, sounding wistful. "You're right. If you just sling them off to any old body you are being disrespectful. I gave my mother's treasures to people who knew her and wanted something to remember her. I'm honored that you trust me with your treasures, Hagen, and thank you."

"Take the bag, too. I would like to be rid of everything in here. The way you transformed downstairs has proved that it's time I moved on."

She picked up the bag, and wearing the coat she proceeded toward the stairs. "I'm moving on, too. Tonight seemed to be the start to a whole new beginning. I could count on my left hand how many dates I've been on in the past six years, and tonight, I had a worthy offer. It pays to be an event coordinator, that's for sure."

"A date?" Trying to sound lightly entertained, he followed her down the stairs. "Morgan, I'm guessing."

"Not a bad guess, since he was the only single male, other than you," she said, turning to smile delightedly at him. "We have a lot in common. He reads for relaxation and we like the same food. I'll just nip into the kitchen and get my bag."

He waited in the hallway beside the bag he had given her, finding that the thought of her with Morgan did not please him one bit. If she planned to throw herself away, she could throw herself in his direction. He had more money than Morgan and, though the point was moot, possibly more class. As well, she liked his family, who certainly liked her.

When she returned, he raised his head, keeping his expression neutral. "You can't choose a man because he reads. He has to, because of his job. You decorate, but you wouldn't want him to be interested in you because you have a good color sense." He moved toward the front door, knowing he sounded as peeved as he felt.

She shrugged and picked up the new bag. "Of course I would. Every time I enter someone's house, I automatically redecorate in my head. I can't help myself. My mind also moves furniture to other spots, too, in almost everyone's house."

He studied the expression of challenge on her face. "That's interesting to hear. I've been pondering about having someone look over this house with a view to redecoration. The success of your dinner set gave me the idea that my entire house should be redone as a tribute to the history of the place. Would you consider taking the job?"

"Do you want your house furnished in antiques?" Her forehead creased.

"No, not entirely, but I would like to see a nod to the house's heritage."

She hesitated. "I would really love to do that, but I have a full-time job at present. After Christmas I would be free." She buttoned the coat all the way down, and snuggled the collar to her face as if savoring the soft fabric. The color complemented her hair color and her face softened with pleasure.

"I would like it finished for Christmas," he said, lingering over his words, and congratulating himself for finding a way to interest her. "Perhaps I could redeploy you."

"You can't do that." Her tone heightened with indignation. "I have a million things I need to do at AA. Tiggy would be devastated if I didn't turn out to be reliable. I have to finish the jobs I started and keep up with the others. But I tell you what"—she stared into his eyes—"I could mock up the design during my days off." Her nose wrinkled. "But I can't for a few weeks. I need to renovate a room in my own house and if I don't finish before the summer arrives, I'll put myself a year behind."

He placed his hand on the doorknob. "What do you need to do?"

"Strip wallpaper, strip paint, sand, and then paint. I want to move into the main bedroom."

"I'll make a deal with you. I'll help you if you help me."

She laughed. "I'm willing to bet you've never painted a room in your life, let alone stripped wallpaper and painted."

"If my sisters can do it, I'm sure I can, too. Do we have a deal?"

She stared at him, her tawny eyes narrowed with calculation. "A room for a room?"

"Is that fair? You only have to plan my rooms, but I have to physically labor in yours."

"I'll have to shop for you, too," she said with a small amount of heat. "I think it will be fair. We could count hours spent and make it fair."

He opened the door and let her through. "In that case," he said, following her outside, "I think we've made a deal. I'll bring your plates back about one, and I'll be dressed as a laborer."

She dinged her car door unlocked, and he walked out onto the street to open it for her. Edging past him, she tossed her two bags onto the car seat and slid into the car. He watched her leave, triumphant. Finally, he had found a way to spend time with her.

* * * *

The bright morning light filtered into the room, reflecting a white glimmer onto the tabletop. Marigold dumped her weekly bags of goods onto her kitchen counter and swiftly unpacked. Since Hagen was about to arrive in barely over two hours, she wondered if she ought to prepare lunch for him.

She decided to eat early and if he hadn't eaten that would be his problem. Eating would waste good working time. She doubted he would last a full afternoon stripping wallpaper, anyway, unaccustomed as he was to physical labor. He would manage a couple of hours at best, though even that would be a great help.

After she had filled her fridge, she hurried out to the car and brought in the paint can, sandpaper, and brushes. Her adviser at the hardware store had recommended sugar soap to remove the wallpaper lining. When she had eaten a quick snack, she made up the solution in a bucket of warm water. She could have hired a steaming machine, but the less money she spent, the better. If all else failed, she would send Hagen off to pick one up while she worked.

She changed into old jeans and an older shirt and began ripping off the top layer of wallpaper. At this rate, she wouldn't finish a single wall until next Easter. Eventually the doorbell rang and she ushered Hagen, dressed in old jeans and a rather nice denim shirt, into her mother's bare bedroom. Scraps of torn wallpaper lay on the floor as witness to her mad effort to finish the job as quickly as possible.

"So, we're ripping off the paper?" Hagen stared at her puny effort. "Don't we have a more efficient way of doing this?"

She made a face of deliberate tolerance. "We strip off the vinyl layer and then we wet the lining paper and scrape that off."

"We can't do it all in one go?" He picked off a piece of lining paper.

"You can try, but this is the way the man in the paint shop told me how to do it."

He glanced at her and turned back to the wall, beginning to rip off long lengths of vinyl. When she looked at her little scraps she was very disappointed with herself. She wanted to be able to do at least one thing better than Hagen. "You must have found the easy part of the wall," she said with no grace.

"We'll swap then." His face a picture of patience, he moved over to her wall and began to tear off almost whole lengths.

"I hate you," she said with no heat. "You remind me of Hubbell Gardiner. Life came easily to him, too."

"Who?"

She shook her head with disappointment. "Morgan would know who Hubbell was. He was the hero in *The Way We Were*, an old weepy I still love."

"If a film makes you weep, why do you love it?" He moved to the next wall and stripped the bleeding, bloody thing almost bare.

She was pleased to see that he hadn't been able to move the lining paper as well. "It's kind of satisfying to have a good cry once in a while."

"This is one of the reasons why men will never understand women."

She stood, staring at his back view, noting the width of his shoulders and the sinews in his bare forearms. The sight of him with rolled-up sleeves made her belly clench with the ache of helpless desire. He had always had a gorgeous male body—tall and broad at the shoulders and slim at the hips. His golden-tanned skin made him perfect. "And a good thing, too." To distract herself from wanting a man she could never have, she started off a shaky rendition of the song, but not being Barbra Streisand she eventually warbled to a stop.

Hagen laughed. "That's pretty awful. No wonder you cried the whole way through."

She sighed loudly. "I'll leave you to rip off the vinyl while I wet the lining. It will need to soak through for a while."

Using long brush strokes, she sugar-soaped most of the first wall, by which time he had finished removing the top layer of vinyl. After she gave a detailed description of the items in her back shed, he came back with the ladder and took over from her, reaching high to the top part of the wall. "Pass me the scraper, and I'll get this lining off while I'm up here."

"I think we need to wait a while for the solution to soak through," she said, raising her eyebrows.

Apparently not. Hagen ignored her instructions, as always. The soggy lining practically fell off the wall in long lengths in his hands, peeling off the bottom layers with the hanging weight. "I now double hate you," she muttered darkly as a damp streamer landed on her head and stuck to her hair.

"You're far too competitive," he said in a companionable voice. "That might have been handy on the swimming team but working together rather than competing is more useful in this situation."

"I'm not competing. I'm simply trying to show you that I am competent."

"Has it ever occurred to you that I am, too?"

"No. You just are. Everyone knows that. You couldn't be a golden boy if you had faults."

He laughed. "I'm amazed to hear I have no faults. Why don't you go and boil the kettle for a nice cup of tea while I finish this?"

"Because I won't be shunted off to do a so-called woman's job so that you can be manly." She planted her fists on her hips.

He turned and grinned at her. "I wouldn't call you a so-called woman. You are definitely a woman, obstinate, and cranky. If you would rather finish this while I rummage around your kitchen trying to find cups and what-all, that's okay by me."

"I wouldn't and you know that. I'll make a cup of tea while you be a man."

"I'll be one whether you make a cup of tea or not." He turned his back on her again.

"I know. And you always have to have the last word," she said as she huffed out of the bedroom, making sure *she* had the last word.

She pulled a couple of stools up to the countertop and placed two mugs of tea on the laminate, already knowing he didn't take milk or sugar. "Tea's ready," she called. "I hope you've finished, Superman."

"One last scrape and done, Lois." He strode along the passage, confident and masculine without a hair on his golden head disturbed. "We'll have time for the first coat of paint today at this rate."

"Oh, joy. Have you painted before?"

"I've done a brush stroke here and there. I'm sure it's not difficult. I might find an instruction or two on the paint can." He widened his eyes in a gormless way.

She sighed loudly. "I'm absolutely sure that your confidence in yourself is not misplaced. Painting this wall will be the same breeze to you that everything else is."

"Not everything." He stood perfectly still, his softened gaze meeting hers. "You are more like a gale."

"Let's not get into times past, Hagen. We were doing so well."

His gaze flickered and the blink of his eye said subject ended. "I have the idea that we might have to wash the wall before we start to paint. How about if I do that while you prepare the brushes, or whatever needs to be done?"

"I can't leave you with the dirty work."

"Yes, you can. You might not understand, but it's doing me the world of good. I don't have to think. I simply need to do. It's therapeutic."

"Go ahead," she said, waving him off. "I wouldn't want to deprive you in that case."

Trying to remember why they were wrong for each other, she turned her back on him while he walked into the bedroom. He might have been her crush since she was sixteen, but even then she knew he needed a feminine, helpless woman who would stand around admiring him, not that Marigold couldn't do that as well. She simply thought she owed it to him and herself that she shared the load. But what would she know? She was the product of a dysfunctional marriage, and he was the product of a successful one. If she'd had half a brain, she would have learned from him rather than try to fight him every step of the way.

Collecting the sandpaper from the pack she had left in the kitchen, she followed him. He held the handle of the bucket of sugar-soap solution in one hand and the big sponge in the other. His arm swept over the wall, swishing steadily.

She kneeled and began to sand down the skirting boards.

"Are you going to do that by hand?" he asked in an interested voice.

"I don't know a way to do it with my foot."

"Don't you have an electric sander?"

"No."

"Are you going to sand down the floor boards or install carpet?"

She worried at a bump of thick paint. "Sand. I want polished floor boards in here, the same as before."

"Then you'll want to sand the floor boards around the edges, too. Stop doing that the hard way. I have an electric sander. I'll run home and get it. Are we planning on painting the walls tonight?"

"What are you? Some kind of masochist? I've barely done an inch of this skirting board and you want me to start on the edges of the floor." She frowned up at him.

"If you want this room done this weekend, you'll need a plan." He stepped down from the ladder. "You continue washing the walls while I get the sander. We'll do the first coat on the wall tonight after a quick meal. Tomorrow Kell will come and sand the floors. I'll get the edges done and that will save him time."

"Kell will sand the floors," she repeated in a tone of disbelief. "I don't happen to owe him a single favor. I can't ask him to do that for me."

"I can. If he has other plans for tomorrow morning, I'll find out and he'll have to do the floor another day."

Open-mouthed, she watched him slide his phone out of his pocket and call Kell. He turned his back on her while he spoke. "Hagen here. Do you have plans for tomorrow morning?" He laughed. "No, I want you to go to AA's workshop and pick up the floor sander. Marigold needs help with a floor." He listened. "Yes, I'm sure Calli will find something to do. I'm planning on being at Marigold's house around nine tomorrow. I'll get the windows covered up. Right. See you."

"I was going to sand the floor myself. I don't really have the money to pay someone to work for me on a weekend," Marigold said, totally embarrassed.

"He and Calli are only too pleased to help. The company owns the floor sander so there won't be any cost to you. However, we need to do as much as we can tonight in prep. The floor dust takes a day to settle and so you won't be able to paint tomorrow. If we can, we'll finish tonight."

"I didn't know you had an electric sander," she said in a robot voice as he wiped his wet hands down the sides of his jeans. She couldn't quite handle how he had taken over. Not having to sand the floors herself was a great relief but everything was moving too fast for her, and now Hagen was organizing her. She never did take well to having someone telling her what to do. Next he would be mansplaining and she would clock him one. "But, by all means get it. And I'll take over washing the walls while you're gone. Unfortunately, we won't have time to paint the room tonight." She lifted her chin.

He gave her a glance of tolerance and he actually drove to his house two streets away while she washed the walls with the long-handled floor sponge. She had almost finished when he arrived back with two electric sanders, reams of sandpaper, and a large can of ceiling white. "I thought finishing the ceiling first might be smart," he said with an apologetic smile. "And I had this in the garage, left over."

She groaned. "Getting the walls of this room painted seemed like simple exercise to me yesterday. You've made it into a full production."

"You don't want to start something that you're not prepared to do properly." He plonked his hands on his hips and stared a challenge at her.

"What's the time?"

"Half past four."

"Right. So, I'll paint the cornices and you can do the rolling of the ceiling. We should be finished in a couple of hours."

In the end, they finished layering two coats on the ceiling in about an hour and a half.

Chapter 6

Hagen hammered on the paint can lid while Marigold folded the sheets they'd used to protect the flooring. "We need to re-energize before we start on the walls." He glanced at her.

One side of her mouth lifted in a smile. "It doesn't matter if I don't get the walls done this weekend. I'll still be ahead because the floor will be done. I can do the rest of the painting next weekend instead, or maybe during the week if I can get myself organized."

Which was not the answer he wanted. Although he knew she didn't have a previous engagement, he wasn't sure that she would go out for a meal with him. She had made her feelings quite clear about not dating him six years ago. If he said anything about a meal, she would see that as a date—unless he could keep his manner casual. At this stage of his life, an out and out rejection from Marigold might start off a series of events that would put him back to square one. "What about a quick meal at the local pub? No prep, no dishes, and then we can finish the walls tonight."

She looked doubtful. "Tempting, but I'm a mess. I don't think I have the energy to get dressed up."

He examined her, carefully performing the disinterested act he had once had down pat, the way he had treated her long ago, before she grew old enough for him to romance. "You're not a mess. You've got wallpaper in your hair and paint on your shirt but if you change your top you'll look presentable."

"Wallpaper?" Leaning over, she ruffled her hair with both her hands, worrying out the dust and the scraps. The back of her neck looked soft and white and entirely too vulnerable. "Better?"

He nodded. "So, that would be a yes?"

She whooshed out a breath. "Okay. That would be far easier than trying to get together something to eat. I hadn't expected to finish the whole room in one day but now that we're almost there, I'd rather keep going. If you're sure you don't mind being seen with a woman who looks like a laborer?"

She looked as much like a laborer as a cat looked like a lion. He smiled. "So, change your shirt and we're off."

She came out of her bedroom at the far end of the hallway, wearing the dark blue knit he had put in her bag yesterday, and she detoured into the bathroom. When she came out, her hair had been brushed into an autumn haze and collected into a mass of curls at the back. He turned away, certain that his expression would show how much he desired her, and he led the way to the front door.

She followed. "I hope we're going in your car. I'm more likely to get away with wearing old jeans if I swing out of a Porsche."

"You clearly think that I'll be parking in the bar. Sorry to tell you, but I have to use the car park like everyone else."

"My confidence comes from my thoughts, not my reality."

He laughed, shaking his head. The drive took about five minutes and being early on a Saturday night gave them a table and quick service. He had some sort of pasta dish and she had the same, washed down with a glass of red wine. Although he would have liked to dally with her, she clearly wanted to get back to work.

By around ten that night, they had painted her new bedroom with two coats of a medium shade of blue. He drove home satisfied. She was expecting him early tomorrow morning, and he couldn't ask for more than that.

When he arrived the next day, Kell's white pickup stood outside the house. The front door currently ajar, Hagen entered the dark hallway, hearing the voices of two women. Not unexpectedly, Calli had arrived to help, too. "Morning," he said as he entered the kitchen where the others stood. "I thought I was early, but apparently not. Nice to see you here, too, Calli."

His sister stood on tiptoe to kiss him on the cheek. She wore jeans and a khaki shirt, clearly prepared to work. "I thought if you could be useful, I could be, too. We brought over a can of floor sealer but I didn't know what else might be needed. But if Marigold is glossing her floors, she will need a carpet square and she is dubious about us finding one in the warehouse that might be good enough for her."

Marigold gasped, and plunked her fists on her hips. "If that's not a twisted tale, I don't know what is. I was telling her that I can't possibly raid your staging supplies for my own use."

"Most of our carpets have a limited life," Hagen said, mentally blessing Calli for her idea. "Quite a few are off-cuts, hemmed, and others we bought from auction houses for a few dollars. None are valuable. They're chosen for their colors, which makes them too memorable to be dragged out too often. If we can't resell them after a certain time, we throw them out."

Calli sent him a glance of gratitude before settling her gaze back on Marigold. "So, if you take one, you would be doing us a favor by contributing one less article to landfill."

"I know," Marigold said drily. "The same favor I'm doing you by letting you spend your Sunday sanding my floor and the same favor I'm doing you by accepting your free paint leftovers." She made the air quotes. "You Allbrooks are hard to match, and I'll never be able to pay you back for all the nice things you do for me."

"Idiot," Calli said, hugging her. "You pay us back in a thousand ways that you don't even notice. Ma told me about the dinner set. It was the hit of the evening on Friday, and it was your idea and your dinner set. You didn't have to do that. And that's only a small example of your generosity. Now we've got the carpet settled, let's go and choose one. We can leave the guys to do their stuff here without our supervision."

"That's if you don't mind us being in your house without you?" Hagen began rolling up his sleeves.

"I'm happy to be elsewhere while the floor is being sanded. So, see you later." She turned and hooked her hand under Calli's arm.

With a toodle-oo twiddle of her fingers and a cheeky smile, Calli led Marigold from the room.

"Let me get the sander out of the car first," Kell said, following behind the ladies. "You'll want the tray top if you're moving carpets. The Porsche isn't big enough."

Kell returned back into the house with the sanding machine. "I had a look at the floor before you arrived," he said to Hagen who was checking last night's paint finish in the bedroom. "It's never had wall-to-wall carpeting, therefore we won't find nails everywhere. We'll want to fill a few gaps, but we can get this job knocked off in an hour or so."

"Did you bring filler?"

"I've brought everything. Good to see you sanded the edges. You're not just a pretty face."

"When your parents run a construction company, you tend to be handy." Hagen grinned at Kell. "Though, Marigold taught me how to strip wallpaper and paint yesterday. I let her. She's rather earnest at times."

Kell smiled back. "You've known her for a long time. I've only known her since I married Calli. I think she's kind of earnest, too, but I wouldn't have thought she was your type."

Hagen pushed his hands into his pockets. "I didn't say she was."

Kell stared at him but made no comment. In silence, they filled the cracks between the floorboards. Hagen blocked out the window while Kell loaded the sanding disks onto the machine, and he went on with the job after Hagen shut the door. With the loud whine of the motor reverberating in his ears, he had little to do while Kell was sanding. Tempted to glance around Marigold's house, he didn't resist.

Her tiny bedroom was one of two singles, separated by the only bathroom, and built at the back of the house. The early fifties construction would have been contracted by her maternal grandparents. In those days, just after the Second World War, builders and supplies were scarce. Too many young and healthy tradesmen had been lost overseas, too few had been trained in the meantime, and the many houses built for those who returned were over-constructed by amateurs. As Hagen knew, knocking one over to repurpose the land was like tearing down a bunker. Often, the only part worth salvaging was the flooring. When she left this place, sure as heck the house would be demolished, having been built in a good area on a generous-sized block.

The third bedroom had been set up as a craft room, holding a sewing machine, rolls of fabric neatly stacked, and labeled boxes on shelves. Her sitting room was also neat but old fashioned. The couch would have been at least twenty years old and her television set was small. Anyone could see nothing had been spent on this house in years.

He wanted her to be more comfortable, but short of helping her renovate, his hands were tied. She wouldn't, he knew from bitter experience, accept handouts. Sighing, he texted Calli. *M needs QS bed. Get AA discount at Choose to Snooze.*

When the dust settled, he swooshed the first coat of sealer on the floors, while Kell fixed the leaky tap in the kitchen.

* * * *

"What do you think of this one?" Calli unrolled one of the bigger carpet pieces, navy blue with a pattern in white.

Marigold stood, watching the zigzags slowly reveal. "That's not bad. I think I would get away with the angled lines. The patches on the quilt are varicolored and multi-patterned triangles set into a darkish blue background.

The colors my mother used will give the bed a starring role. I'll probably make a white blind and have sheer white linen either side of the window."

"Sounds good." Calli began to roll up the carpet again. "That was quicker than I thought. Now for a bed."

"I've got a bed."

Calli grinned. "You've got a single bed. Your new room will look far better with a bigger one. I think you're grown up enough to qualify for a bed you might like to share occasionally."

"I suppose that could happen one day. At least I've begun dating. Well, that doesn't happen until Friday but it's a start, at least."

"Who?" With a delighted expression on her face, Calli grabbed her arm.

"Morgan Evans, a prof from the engineering department at the uni."

"Oh, good." Calli moved away and lifted one end of the carpet. "Pick up that end, and we'll get it into the car. Then we'll go off to Choose to Snooze. We can get a huge discount there but they also have lower prices on Sundays. Don't look like that. You must have been paid and the bed will cost almost nothing, I promise. So, Morgan Evans, huh? I don't know him. What's he like?"

Marigold followed Calli carrying the front end of the carpet. "A bit taller than me and a bit older. Quite nice looking and clever, book clever. I don't know how much we'll have in common, but if I don't try out a few guys I'll never know if one might suit me."

"You certainly have to check out Morgan. If all else fails, you ought to get a good meal." Calli pushed open the loading door of the warehouse with her foot.

"That was my caveat, too, but, well, he's interesting. I'm rather keen on brainy guys. Hold on. I need to take the step more slowly. I can't see where my feet are."

Calli turned back to wait for her. "Speaking of brainy guys, I love that you're getting Hagen interested in something other than work."

"I don't know that I am. He had to help me because he wants me to help him and if he doesn't, I won't have time. I need to get this room done before Christmas. And he wants his house done before Christmas, too." Marigold huffed a little as Calli paced quickly to Kell's car.

"He's redoing the house? Fantastic! Far be it from me to speak ill of the dead, but that house was furnished by Mercia whose ideas came from pictures of the houses of movie stars."

Marigold laughed. "Well, she was kind of a movie star herself. I think the house suited her."

"I do, too." Calli put down her end of the carpet so that she could open the back of the tray top. As soon as the door swung down, she grabbed the carpet. She and Marigold stuffed the roll in with much huffing and puffing. "But it's a good sign that Hagen's ready to move along."

"It's not as easy as you might think to stop grieving for someone you love." Calli gave a helpless gesture with a lift of her hands. "I know. I haven't experienced losing any of the people I love. Hagen's still young enough to find someone else. As an onlooker, I don't want him to mourn forever."

"No one does that. He already has a divorcee chasing him."

Calli nodded. "Scarlett. I think she was keen on him while Mercia still was alive." She walked around to the driver's seat.

Marigold took the passenger seat and let herself be driven to buy a new bed. She did need one, and she could afford one, but being economical was a hard habit to break. Fortunately, the price of the bed and a comfortable mattress, with an AA discount, worked out to be about half the price she had imagined. "I'll have to go shopping with you more often," she said happily to Calli on the way home.

"You certainly will. What are you going to do about furniture in that room?"

"Aha. I have my mother's cupboard in the shed, waiting to be done up. It's a beauty with a set of drawers down on one side. It's authentic fifties and it will look just right once I have painted and restored it."

"You don't want a built-in?" Calli pulled out of the car park, concentrating on the traffic she meant to join.

"Maybe one day, but for now what I have is okay. I don't need luxury. Just comfort."

"I hope the guys have been working hard. I don't want to get back and find out that they're not ready for lunch."

"Is it that time already?" Marigold glanced at the car clock. "I don't have much food in the house. Would you mind stopping off somewhere so that I can buy something?"

"Well...I was hoping you and Hagen would come with us to Kell's brother's place for lunch."

"The one who married Vix Tremain?"

"They like to do family things and when we said we were helping you today, Vix asked if we would ask you, too."

"Me? Or Hagen?"

"Both. Vix used to have a crush on Hagen at school, or so she said."

"Didn't everyone?"

"You didn't."

"The competition was too heavy for me," Marigold said, hoping the warmth of her cheeks would be attributed to the car's heater rather than show that in those days she wasn't as casual about Hagen as his sisters supposed. "Plus, he was your brother. How awkward that would have been!"

Calli gave a noncommittal smile. "I think we could have forgiven you a letch or two. It seemed unnatural that two people who had so much in common had no interest in each other."

Marigold had nothing to say to that. Everyone had known that Hagen's main interest when he'd left for his university college had little to do with study. Each time she had seen him he had been with a different girl. He was hardly about to engage her in conversation when he had one of his vegan, gluten-free girlfriends to placate about his mother's delicious Greek cuisines.

Soon enough, Calli pulled the car up outside Marigold's house. The guys had put the first coat of sealer on the floor, after waiting for the dust to settle, and Hagen said the second coat could be done later in the afternoon.

"And my new bed will arrive tomorrow," Marigold said to him with some satisfaction. "I'll have to leave the key with next door because I won't be home."

"I thought you were taking off tomorrow." Hagen frowned at her.

"I already said I wouldn't. I have to choose new carpeting for the Rundle Street apartment block and haggle about the new reception chairs. I might need to swap around a few pictures as well. It seems a better idea to change the whole area rather than just replace the worn out things, and we have plenty of pictures in the warehouse that are dying to have an outing."

"They communicate with you, do they?"

"So to speak." She grinned.

"I don't know if Kell asked you, Hagen," Calli said tentatively. "But we're off to Jay's house for lunch. You're invited, too. Marigold is coming."

Hagen glanced at Marigold. "Sure. I can't do much more here. I might go home and change out of these dusty clothes. I'll pick you up, Marigold."

She nodded. He always looked better than anyone had a right to look. For a lunch he would dress in something smart but casual in exactly the right colors. Fortunately, at a family lunch where every other woman was married, she wouldn't have any competition so that during the next couple of hours she could fantasize that she was his chosen date. Already her insides had gone into meltdown.

She straightened her shoulders and stared directly at Hagen, keeping her tone more on the friendly side than on the wishful side. "Before you leave, could you and Kell bring in the wardrobe from the garage?"

He raised his eyebrows at Kell, who nodded.

"Thanks, guys. I'll paint it sometime during the week and use it in my new bedroom. Put it in the passage outside the dining room," she called to the two retreating furniture movers. Then she shrugged at Calli. "No point in wasting muscle power."

Calli laughed. "I love seeing Hagen out of office mode and no longer the property prince."

"He's not bad when he takes off his suit." Marigold made a mock lecherous expression, waggling her eyebrows, too overdone to be taken seriously. She cleared her throat. "So to speak."

Calli nodded. "So to speak."

The job duly performed, the others left, Calli making sure her brother knew where Jay and Vix lived. Marigold put on clean jeans and the cream top Hagen had given her. Best not to overdress when everyone else at the lunch could buy and sell her ten times over.

* * * *

After a satisfying and companionable lunch with Calli's husband's interesting family, Hagen slid into his car beside Marigold, wondering if his day with her would end as soon as he had sluiced the second coat of sealer onto her floor. He hoped not. The more time he could spend with her, the more he could see that if she had ever been an ice-maiden, not a trace remained. She was no longer rigid in her opinions, set in her ways, or as unlikely to misbehave.

Like him, she had been left without the main focus of her life. Humanity had grabbed hold of her and, with luck, wouldn't let go. He had always suspected that if she stopped dismissing him as rich and irresponsible, she would find out that he wasn't as shallow as she thought.

"Vix hasn't changed, has she?" He smoothly transitioned his car into the end-of-weekend traffic, which wasn't too different from peak hour in the weekday mornings.

"She was in your year at school. You would know her better than me, but I always thought she was nice—one of those quiet achievers."

"Except at Calli's and Kell's wedding, I hadn't seen her in years. She was at uni with me, but she married young and we lost touch."

"I lost touch with most people a few years ago, except for your family. It got too hard trying to fit in friends and earn a living."

He changed into the left lane. "While looking after your mother?"

"She would have done the same for me," she said in defensive voice.

"Any parent would do that for her child. Not every child would do that for her parent. I had no idea, back then, that you were about to be her home caregiver." He hadn't meant to voice those words aloud and he wished them back. Yet, at some time he needed to confront the past. During the last few days, he had forgiven himself for Mercia's death and he wanted to turn back the clock on his life to pre-Mercia days.

For a moment she sat unmoving, while the air between them made a space that begged to be filled. "I was twenty," she finally said. "A young twenty. The whole thing was growing hot and heavy too fast."

"That's what happens in relationships."

"I didn't have time for a relationship. I needed to be my mother's support."

"That's easy for you to say," he said, trying to sound casual. "I never expected you to walk out on me without any explanation. You didn't give a thought to my ego."

"I thought it was large enough to sustain you."

He glanced out the side window. "Maybe these days, but then I thought I was hot stuff."

"I was just another warm body to you."

"Of course you weren't. I had known you for years."

"I couldn't maintain a relationship with anyone, Hagen. It wasn't you. It wasn't me. It was the situation. We had nothing going for us. You were being supported by your parents, and I was working to supporting mine. How could that work?"

"What should I say? Thank you for sparing me?"

"You could, yes." Her laugh sounded dour.

"I can't, of course." He tried for a smile as he pulled up at a red light. "I don't have your sort of grace."

"Grace? Is that a mixture of love and duty? I'm sure if you had been in the same situation you would have done the same, but you weren't. Your sisters unwittingly kept me up to scratch with your life. Within weeks of you trying to get me into your bed, apparently you suddenly started to date every woman who blinked at you. Date is a euphemism, but the word they used. If I happened to hear about it on the grapevine, they didn't want me to be shocked about their brother's extreme sex life."

"And were you?" He lifted an eyebrow at her.

She turned away and stared out the window of the car. "Not shocked, no. I always thought you were a player. I was more shocked by my own behavior."

He glanced at her. "Shocked that you'd been so adamant about not seeing me again."

"Shocked that after only two dates and a couple of kisses that I had raced back to your college rooms to have sex with you."

"And what about you? How was your sex life after refusing me?"

"None of your business."

"What if I want to make it my business?"

"What's that supposed to mean? You brag about yours, and I apologize about mine? Stuff you, Hagen. You, at least, had Mercia."

"At least I had Mercia." He tightened his fingers on the steering wheel and bit out his next words. "Which seemed like the right thing to do at the time." An ache filling his chest, he stared straight ahead at the lines of traffic. At the next set of lights, he would turn left up Kensington Road and drive to her house to finish her damned floor.

To be with her, the woman he'd never had, for a full day had been physical agony. In fact, he'd had a half erection for two weeks. He flicked a quick glance at her and noted her stillness. She had wrapped her hands together, and she stared into her lap, blinking hard. He'd as good as told her he still wanted her and all she could do was tell him he was lucky to have had Mercia—about as lucky as owning a million dollar note. He breathed out, trying to relax his shoulders. "Are you deliberately ignoring my last suggestion?"

"To pry into my sex life?"

"In a manner of speaking. I want to make your sex life my business, if you will let me. This wouldn't be the most subtle proposition you've ever had, but given that we're sitting in a car in the middle of peak hour traffic, it's the best I can do."

"Well, you're a man in a hurry. I shouldn't expect chocolates and roses."

"I suspect you would rather have a sealed floor and new front gate."

"Damn you, Hagen. You know I would."

"So, if handyman porn turns you on, first I'm going to get you back home, and then I'm going to put the last coat of sealer on your floor. What happens after that, well, it's up to you, but I think I should buy us pizza and we should discuss the matter."

She sat silent. He couldn't look at her. If she planned to reject him all over again, he wanted the words over and done with. He needed to know he had no hope. He needed to go on with the rest of his life.

"Did you bring condoms?"

"What!"

"You heard. I'm not currently using contraception."

His breath stilled. "I haven't used a condom for years. Of course I didn't bring any. How confident do you assume I am?"

"This is why I asked." She carefully unfurled her hands, spreading one on each of her thighs.

He waited for the lights to change and, his jaw ticking with tension, he sped across, whipping over two lanes to get to the outside. "The time is now four-thirty and the pharmacist at the shopping mall will close at five. Please excuse my haste."

"I'm pleased to see how enthusiastic you are."

He covered her closest hand with his. She snaked her thumb out and caressed his skin before he needed both hands on the wheel. The hole in his chest filled with warmth, and he didn't know how he had gotten away with any of his words. When she wanted to be prickly, she could be an echidna but when she wanted to be warm she was hot.

Today luck was with him and as his car muttered through the car park he spotted a space right outside the double glass doors of the pharmacy. He parked and shot inside, checking his back pocket for his wallet. A woman stood by the cash register. "Good afternoon. I'm after a packet of condoms."

She looked unfazed. "What size?"

He mulled saying king sized and his lips twitched. "Average, I suppose."

"Colors?" She turned to the shelf behind. "Any preferences."

He rubbed his chin. "Something generic will do. I don't suppose you sell chocolates and roses here."

"You'll find them in the supermarket at the end of the mall." Her mouth ticked into a smile.

He glanced around the shop. "Let me find a substitute." Lying right in front of him on the counter was a rose-pink umbrella that folded to the size of a hand. Then on a cosmetic counter two steps away, he saw a bottle of the perfume that looked classy enough to buy for Marigold. On the way back, he picked up jellybeans in boxes and transparent bags. He handed the lot to the assistant who happily took his credit card. She started packing everything.

"Don't put the condoms in the bag. I'll take them, minus the box." He had the idea he was making the assistant's day. Her mouth widened with enjoyment while he removed the cardboard box and stuffed the packs of condoms into his back pocket.

"Enjoy," she said with a smile as she handed him his bag of goodies. Gripping the handles tightly, he hurried back to the car.

He opened the driver door and slid in, placing the bag onto Marigold's lap. "For you."

"Condoms? Judging by the weight of this bag, I'm going to have a wearying time meeting your expectations." Marigold stared at the bag, looked at him, and gave a spluttering, overwhelmed, half-hysterical laugh.

"Likely, after all the years of abstinence, I won't live up to my expectations, either."

"All the years?"

"Stress is making me exaggerate." He started the engine and turned to glance out the back window while he backed out of the parking space.

"I would be interested to know what you have to be stressed about."

"The condoms, for a start. I have no idea what I bought. Apparently, I'm supposed to know my size and discuss it with a strange woman who will then hand over my color and design preference."

"What color did you buy?"

"I'm hoping you will find out eventually."

"Your whole proposition was so strangely unemotional that I'm sorely tempted."

He turned and grinned at her. "I think you might find that only my words are unemotional. The rest of me is amazingly reinvigorated."

Chapter 7

Marigold put the bag she had carried inside onto the kitchen counter top, peeled off the sealing tape, and looked inside. Not a condom to be seen. Puzzled for a moment, she stared at Hagen.

He shrugged.

She shook out the bag and a rose-pink umbrella; five boxes of the tiny, tasty jellybeans; two bags of the big glucose sort; and a bottle of an expensive perfume she had craved tumbled out onto the laminate surface. "Well, almost chocolates and roses, or the pharmacy's version of same," she said, laughing. She put her hand on his forearm, lifted up her face, and kissed him on the cheek.

The smell of his skin, an indefinable earthy warmth, brought back memories of his last year at school when he had asked her to dance at the school formal. "This is adorable, Hagen," she said, wanting to rip off the cellophane and squirt herself with a prettier scent than the wine and quiche she'd consumed for lunch.

He'd done something adorable back in those days, too. She'd had a hard time finding a date for that night, and her heart had leaped into her throat when he stood smiling in front of her in the balloon-clustered school gym, the venue for the formal. Calli and Tiggy each had boyfriends and one had found a friend to ask Marigold. The boy hadn't been much interested in her, and as soon as they arrived at the formal, he had dragged her onto the dance floor and performed his version of a cool rap all around her, while she moved from foot-to-foot wondering how stupid she looked.

Apparently, too stupid, and he didn't bother with her from then on. She stood in a girl-group for a while, watching the in-crowd dance, while she wondered why the sophomores had compulsory lessons on how to waltz and perform the fox trot. She had practiced each of those alone at home.

Probably half way though the evening, Hagen appeared in front of her. "I don't suppose you can waltz?"

If she hadn't been frazzled by feeling like a dork all night in the awful dress her mother had found for her to wear, she might have been more polite to him. He was, after all, the school captain, and she should have been honored. Instead, she was hurt that, although she had known his family for a couple of years, he hadn't had the courtesy to talk to her for quite a while. "I'm pretty certain you can't," she said with an upward tilt of her nose, aching inside because she thought he was gorgeous and he thought she was a kid.

"There's a challenge." He offered his confident smile. No one could tamp the golden boy down. Grabbing her hands, he pulled her onto the floor. "I'm supposed to be setting an example, but my date can't waltz. I suspected Old Money could."

She aimed a resentful glance at him. "You're not supposed to notice we sophomores exist."

"Mainly I don't, but you're in my home day and night. I would have to be blind not to notice you. Your hair is the color of marigolds." He had laughed.

"Weird, when that happens to be my name." And then she couldn't talk because he moved her into a wild waltz all around the edges of the room.

People stopped to stare at the strange couple who had clearly lost any decorum they might have possessed. Marigold started laughing like a crazy person, and Hagen joined her. A few of the other seniors started waltzing, too, and then people who didn't know how to do the steps and only wanted to be whirled. Marigold had almost the best ten minutes of her life.

And she realized her crush had turned into a longing she couldn't suppress. The music finished, and he moved back, giving her a courtly bow. She curtsied without feeling like a dork. Being with Hagen did that to a girl: made her think she was some sort of princess.

"See you around," she said.

And he said, "Probably not. You're still jail bait, Marigold, and I would prefer to see you in a year or two."

She had watched him leave and gather his date to chummy up to the school principal. He couldn't do that with a sixteen-year-old sophomore.

The next summer at their beach house, he spent most of his time sailing. By then he had been accepted into the university to study engineering.

And now he was an engineer working for his father in the family company. Hagen's life had been mapped for him long ago, and he had grown up motivated, conscientious, and responsible. Since the first moment she had met him she had realized he was the sort of man she wished her father had been, and the only sort of man she would ever want.

In the meantime, not a thing had changed. He was still all she had ever wanted and even now he hadn't let her down by treating her like a widower's opportunity. When he had put his purchases on her lap in the car, although the bag was too big to be merely holding condoms, she would have been disappointed in him if he had truly been prepared to have convenient sex with her. Instead, he hadn't bought any condoms at all. She moved back and noted his rueful smile.

He took a deep breath. "I'm glad you recognized my apology for propositioning you in such a crass way. I'm not saying I don't want to have sex with you, because I do, but I can see this is neither the time nor the place. And I should do a little wooing first."

"Wooing, Hagen?"

"Uh-huh." He picked up her left hand and brought her palm to his mouth. After placing a soft kiss on her skin, he closed her fingers. "That's to keep. You have a date at the end of the week with Morgan. But after that, perhaps on Saturday night, you would have a date with me?" His gaze questioned her.

"A real date?"

"Real-ish. Would you be interested in a movie?"

"As a matter of fact," she said, holding his precious kiss tightly in her palm, "I would like to see *Love and Friendship*."

"That sounds appropriate."

"You don't know what it is, do you?"

"Nope."

"It's a Jane Austen movie."

"I'm sure I can manage that. Perhaps we could have a casual meal afterwards."

"That's a date. I'm so glad you really didn't buy condoms. It would have been so awkward when I don't have any sort of suitable space in the house to entertain you as your comfort woman."

His eyebrows queried her. "Comfort woman?"

"The one a widower has sex with before he goes out into the world again to meet a rich, beautiful woman he wants to marry."

"I'm not about to do that in any hurry. First, I need to seal your floor." He rolled up his sleeves, smiling at her as if he had all the time in the world.

"I could probably do that myself." She watched him pry open the lid of the glossy paint.

"I'm sure you could, but then you won't owe me a favor, and I won't get my house done in time for Christmas." He grabbed the can and the long-handled wool pad he had used to spread the first coat on the floor. She stood watching him. "Well, I could go out and get pizza."

"You could make us a cup of coffee. I won't take long." He strode to the new blue bedroom while she found mugs and coffee bags and switched on the electric kettle.

And he didn't take long. The kettle had barely boiled before he arrived back in the kitchen. "I think it's easier to throw away the sealer pad than to try to clean it." He untied the mop-head and tossed the matted pad into her kitchen bin. "I don't think you'll need another coat."

"Thanks, Hagen. You've done a great job, and now I owe you a couple of hours of design time."

"Four hours to be exact. Now I'm off the get a pizza," he said drinking his coffee standing up.

She didn't think he would want to eat pizza in the formality of the dining room, so after he strolled out, she put a couple of mats on the kitchen table, glad she didn't have a bottle of wine in the house, or she would be too tempted to make an occasion of this. The sooner he went home, the better, while she was in this sentimental mood about him.

He brought back her favorite margarita pizza, and she wondered if he remembered or if that was his favorite now, too. Eating the pizza together was companionable and when he had gone, she thought about her condom comment. Maybe she wouldn't have minded a bout of recreational sex with him, except for having to face him at work. Fortunately he had changed his mind, or he hadn't been serious. Even more fortunately, he hadn't realized for a minute or two she had been.

Other than with him, she had never contemplated sex with anyone, but she owed it to herself to give another man a chance to impress her—if Morgan intended to try. But when she took the cellophane off the perfume box, and dotted the perfume on her wrists, the fragrance reminded her of Hagen's kiss in her palm, and she wept for all the lost chances and all the lonely years that she had spent wishing she hadn't walked out on Hagen after they had finally, after five years of longing on Marigold's part, gotten together.

* * * *

Hagen settled into his study with his weekend homework in front of him, realizing that he had dodged a bullet. Whether by instinct or pure rat-cunning, he had stored the condoms in his pocket. Marigold hadn't been serious, and he was surprised with himself for thinking she might be. Comfort woman? She had never been that. The one time, six years ago, he'd almost had sex with her had been testing because he had held himself back during two long dates beforehand. To finally get her into his bed, not only willing but also eager, had seemed to be a dream come true. She made no secret of being inexperienced, and he was willing to go slowly and not obey the cravings of his own body.

Okay, so she wouldn't even consent to oral sex, but she had two beautiful breasts and once he had kissed her he hadn't wanted to stop. Even now, he couldn't say why she wasn't like anyone else, but he saw her as twenty times sexier. That night, while he had been basking in his luck to have finally found the right time with the right woman, she was sitting on his bed staring at him, knotting her incredible hair and staring back.

"I have to go home now," she said, her face stiff.

"We haven't done anything, yet," he'd said, on edge.

"That's as much as I'm going to do."

His heart dropped. "What happened?" he asked, puzzled.

"It was an interesting experiment but not an interesting experience."

He had dressed in a daze. He'd been overconfident because she was the sort of woman he wished he could spend his life with, one whose beauty came from within. He doubted he would ever feel the same way again about another woman. When he dropped her off, she told him she would see him from time to time because of his sisters but as far as she was concerned, the episode had never happened.

During the intervening years, he hadn't lost his head with another woman though he had appreciated quite a few. Eventually he had moved on, and he had finally married Mercia. Now he discovered that Marigold's conscientiousness had led her to cut him out of her life. All along she had been planning to be her mother's caregiver. Full time. She hadn't expected to have a life of her own. She had never been anything other than responsible, and he should have known.

Since Mercia's death, going to work had been his way of shutting out his guilt about her. In the past two weeks, he had looked forward to running into Marigold, hearing her odd comments, her sudden laughter, and her opinions about anything she cared to share. The sun in his life finally shone. Now, no matter how difficult, he planned to push his way back into her life.

He opened the door to his office the next morning, cheery rather than dedicated to making a success of himself.

"Morning," Sandra called. "Did you have a good weekend?"
She always asked that, and he said as he always said, "Yes."
"What did you do?"
"Spent time with friends, eating, etcetera."
"How was your dinner?"
"Splendid, Sandra, splendid, the food, the company."
"I thought you were entertaining pollies?"
"And they were entertaining me," he said light heartedly.
Then Marigold strolled in. "Morning, all. Good weekend, Sandra?"
"Lazy and quiet. All around good. I hear your dinner went off well."
"Extra well for me. I got a date out of it. This is a great job. I can't work out why Tiggy disappeared."

"She was having too much fun. She thought she ought to make herself more miserable elsewhere." Sandra slid behind her desk. "That's only a guess, mind you. Maybe she was just sick of work."

"She hardly ever had time off. I think she needed it." Hagen pushed his hands into his pockets. "How about you, Marigold? Did you have a good weekend?"

"Very productive. I painted my new bedroom top to bottom and then I stripped and polished my floor. What did you do, Hagen?" She stood there, her fine eyebrows raised, her eyes expressing silent laughter.

He considered his answer for a moment while his body responded with a thump of desire. "Hot air ballooning in the Barossa followed by visits to a few wineries," he said, expanding on Marigold's flights of fantasy.

"You did not," Sandra said, pushing her spectacles down to the tip of her nose and staring over the top. "You sat at home thinking up ways to keep me busy today."

Hagen sighed. "I'm too predictable, I fear. Perhaps that's a plan for another weekend. Do you believe Marigold painted her whole room?"

Sandra lifted her face and stared at him. "She has paint under her cuticles. I would say she did."

"I can't hide anything from you, I see." Marigold grinned. "While I have your attention, Hagen, may I ask what the budget is for the apartment block reception area?"

"Show me your design and the cost estimates. If the two correlate, we'll see." He backed into his office, wondering how he would keep separate working with Marigold and playing with her. The temptation to romance her in the office was great, but a man who dabbled with his employee, be she a friend of the family or not, was asking for workplace insurrection.

After he had spent some time plotting the agenda of the next board meeting, he phoned one of his contractors about the school block's progress, only to be sidetracked onto the engineering report for the newer part of the build.

He picked up his phone, and called Sandra. "Would you mind bringing me a cup of coffee? I'm snowed under."

"I wouldn't mind, normally, but I'm snowed under, too. I have to get your agenda sent off to everyone right away so that I can have the amendments back within the next hour. Also, the electrical contractor for the school job wants the plans for the new builds. I have to follow up—I'll see if Marigold will get your coffee. She is about to leave for her own."

"No—" But she had hung up. He swung out of his chair and moved to open the door. Marigold didn't see him. She gave Sandra a nod, and she disappeared. Although he had wanted coffee at his desk so that he could finish his current job, if Marigold brought back his drink, he would be distracted. Now placed in the position of waiting for her to distract him, he twiddled his thumbs until she returned.

She practically slithered into his office, two cups of coffee in one hand. "May I have a word? I want to run my ideas by you."

"Plans, Marigold. Not ideas. I'm not artistic like you and Tiggy. I need plans." He rubbed his forehead. At this stage, he had her in his head instead of the worries of the electrical contractor. He sighed. "You may as well bring them to me now. Leave your coffee here."

She plunked both cups on his desk and scooted over to her office, arriving back with a ream of paper. "I've mocked up the area and noted the costs and the colors, but I want to do something extra, which will, of course, cost more."

Shifting the coffees to one side, he placed her pages in front of him, indicating she should continue.

She did. "New carpet, naturally, and that will be measured up after the walls are painted. The painter gave me these quotes and the carpet cost is in this range." She pointed to a line of figures. "I'm having seating made instead of buying it off the showroom floor because this is a classy apartment block, and I think we should be using the place as an advertisement for all your other apartment blocks."

"Of course." He leaned back, examining her earnest expression.

"The seating is along large clean lines, oversized and tailored. I'm using turquoise for the furniture and blush pink accents with tan walls and carpet. See these shapes?" She pointed at a pencil drawing she had done as neatly as her drawing of his house, which she'd had printed onto the place cards for the dinner.

The design looked art deco, which he liked. Until recently, his office had contained an art deco style couch and two chairs in burgundy. Tiggy had changed this to a more modern backless seating arrangement in black to discourage people from taking up too much of his time. "The price?"

"This is the quote." She flipped through a couple of pages. Her perfume suited her, floral and light. He wondered if she wore the perfume he bought for her.

He nodded. "Fair enough. And you're not planning anything outrageously expensive?"

"*Well.* You haven't used artwork in the area, and I understand why. You clearly couldn't use the staging prints in a place this exclusive, and good artwork is expensive. If it was a public space, we could get artists to exhibit their work, but the apartments are privately owned and only the owners would see them, so that's not a great incentive to get any artist to exhibit."

"What's your idea?"

"That we pay money for good artwork." She smiled.

He twisted his mouth wryly. "That sounds economical to you?"

"You're advertising your company, remember? What if you offered an art prize and the winner would have his or her art displayed in the foyer until the next winner the next year?"

"I'll think about it. Your bed is arriving today. Call me if you want a hand setting it up."

"I'm the queen of the bed-screwers. Bad phrasing. I screwed three together in the schoolhouse staging. I did the third in about ten minutes." She groaned. "I'm making it sound worse, but you know what I mean." Her aristocratic nose tilted, and she flicked a speck of imaginary dust from her shoulder.

He kept his amused smile. "So you won't need me?" He tried to sound relieved rather than disappointed, which he was, because he didn't want thoughts of her screwing three men in a schoolhouse to occupy his thoughts. That was more the sort of activity Mercia's friends got up to.

She shook her head. "Not for making up a bed," she said, sounding cryptic. She collected her diagrams and left.

He sat wondering if she had meant to be cryptic or if he merely wanted her to be cryptic. Holding an optimistic thread in his mind, he shifted himself back into work mode and made sense of the engineering report.

The click of his door opening brought his head up. "Scarlett. I didn't hear you knock." He frowned, rising to his feet, hoping to usher the beautiful blonde out before she wasted too much of his time.

"That's because I didn't knock, darling. There's no one out there guarding you, so I thought I would slip in unnoticed."

He suppressed a groan. "A problem with the furniture delivery?"

She shook her head, and half hooded her eyes. He knew why she was here again. She'd thought that after Mercia's death, and the subsequent divorce of her husband, that Hagen and she ought to console each other. "I came to thank you for letting the theater company borrow your furniture. I thought as a reward, I would cook dinner for you tonight at my place."

"That's very kind of you, Scarlett, but it was our pleasure to make a small contribution."

"And making dinner for you tonight will be my pleasure." Scarlett was a discreet woman and his dead wife's best friend. He knew her seductive smiles as well as he knew Mercia's but while she glided toward him, he stood like a rabbit caught in a car's headlights, because he could only think of Marigold. Before he could blink, Scarlett had a one cool hand on the back of his neck and the other heading toward his zipper.

"Not here, Scarlett." Evading her lipstick, he took her seeking hand in his. She settled her body right into him, teasing the lobe of his ear between her teeth. Stuck between her teeth and her thigh across his buttocks, he managed to step sideways. Her foot landed on the floor and his earlobe escaped amputation by a millisecond before Marigold walked past the open door. His palm still rested on Scarlett's waist but he managed to turn her to face the exit.

"Scarlett is just leaving," he said to Marigold. His voice sounded gruff.

"I hope you didn't have a problem with the furniture delivery," Marigold said blinking at Scarlett. Her demeanor said polite patience.

"No problem." Scarlett's expression showed no sign of awkwardness. "I'll speak to you later, Hagen. Don't forget my invitation."

"I won't." After she had gone, he scrubbed his ear with his handkerchief.

* * * *

The week flew by, and then Friday suddenly gave Marigold the jitters. She awoke in the morning dithering about clothes. By this time tomorrow, she would have participated in the first man-date she'd had in a long while. She wished she hadn't worn the gray-and-black dress at Hagen's dinner, for now Morgan had seen her only new outfit.

Then again, because the dress was so neutral, he might not remember she had worn it before. After she arrived home from work, she wriggled into the dress. Knowing blue softened the pink tones of her skin, she added a flowing pale blue scarf. She looked okay, not especially good or bad. Sighing, she twisted her hair into a loose knot at the nape of her neck. Then she pulled out a few curls around her face. She now looked a little less businesslike.

Morgan arrived on time, dressed in beige cotton pants, a white shirt with a brown-striped tie, and a brown suit jacket. With his mild brown eyes and medium brown hair, he looked rather nice. "I have a table booked at that new place on Unley Road," he said, escorting her to his comfortable car.

The place he ushered her into was smart and warm, packed with people about her age who looked very fashionable, the women not wearing as much as she would have expected, given the chilly weather. However, she understood the need to look sexy even if you had goose bumps. She couldn't do that herself but she knew she was fuddy-duddy. A bare midriff in early spring weather wasn't her idea of wise.

Morgan was shown to a good table in a sheltered part of the room and treated to prompt service. He had a placid, confident manner, a healthy smile, and he treated her like a fragile flower. As a responsible woman, she didn't like being treated like a fragile flower. Hagen treated her like a responsible woman.

Although the meal was beautifully presented, she felt as awkward as a thistle in a bed of violets. Morgan ate like a food judge, tasting everything either with smacking appreciation or long consideration as if he was giving a mental score to each morsel he ate. He had a tendency to gesture with his knife while he spoke.

You couldn't take him anywhere, her mother would have said if she had seen that, but Marigold didn't go anywhere so that wouldn't matter.

When she made what she thought were leading comments, which would have baited Hagen into laughing or retaliating, Morgan looked puzzled. He didn't get her sense of humor. Hagen had understood her from the start, and he never fell into her linguistic traps. He gave as much as he took. Morgan didn't fall into them either because he thought she was serious, and he judged her accordingly as a humorless and silly woman. She could see him mentally wishing himself with anyone but her.

"The meal has been wonderful," she said after she finished off every last morsel of her dessert, a collection of tiny tastes of gelato, decorated with almond bread, sugared violets, and micro-strawberries. "That tasted as delicious as it looked. I'll have to recommend this place to everyone I know."

Morgan looked relieved. "The owner is married to my cousin. Your recommendation will help a lot."

"Even without, he is sure to be a success." She folded her hands in front of her, certain she looked ready to leave, and equally certain he didn't mind her having an early night.

He aimed his gaze at the service counter, lifted a finger, and the bill arrived. After producing his credit card, his payment was taken. On the trip back home, the silence begged to be filled, and she did, commenting on food, the weather, the success of the dinner party the week before and anything she could think of to say to this man with whom she had nothing in common.

He walked her to the front door, which was nice of him when his face said he had wasted his time and money. Then all she could say was, "Thank you. The night out was much appreciated."

He nodded and disappeared into the night, and she had the idea she had let herself down. Getting into the dating scene was difficult for a woman her age. At least she had completing her bedroom décor to amuse her tomorrow, before her movie date with Hagen.

He had said he would collect her at four in the afternoon, having decided on the early showing of the movie. She had plenty of time until then to finish off the details in her bedroom. During the week, she had made the linen side curtains which, pulled across the window, gave an amount of privacy inside and fortunately left her with a hazed-over view of the soft pittosporum that grew in front of the side fence.

The next morning, she awoke with a smile. The day had begun, the day she hadn't ever thought would come, the day she had a real date with handsome, hunky, ultra-desirable Hagen.

First, shopping, a small amount of cleaning, fresh sheets—she loved crisp new clean sheets—and then she puttered into the sewing room. Amazingly, she finished her sewing before lunch and then she spent some time later in the afternoon hanging the blind she had made. After that, she sat on the windowsill and stared into the room contemplating the bed.

The décor revolved around her lovely patchwork quilt, made by her dying mother out of memories: a few squares from one of Marigold's baby dresses, pieces of her old school uniform, a repeating pattern made from the curtains she'd had as a child, an old tablecloth, her grandmother's ball gown, long forgotten cushion covers, all cobbled together with borders of dark blue. The pale orange lining was the only part of the quilt that was brand new.

Marigold had used white sheets and pillowcases as a contrast, and the carpet from the AA warehouse looked perfect. A few plain cushions would hold the design together, and she had an old chair she planned to cover to match the lining of the quilt. All she really needed were framed pictures on the walls. She would think about those and meanwhile make the cushion covers.

By three o'clock, she had made three cushion covers, one in aqua blue and two in the pale orange fabric she would use for the chair. The hands of the clock kept moving, and she had no idea what to wear to go to a movie and a meal with Hagen. If she'd had a full wardrobe of clothes, she might have had a choice. As a stay-at-home sewer for many years, she'd had no need to think about dressing for dates. Sighing, she pulled on her black pants and the cream knit top Hagen had given her. She filled the Burberry bag with her purse, clean tissues in case she cried in the movie, a comb, and a lipstick.

Her hair gave her all sorts of problems. She wanted to look good to Hagen. For work she pinned up her hair in various ways. For the movies, she decided on a figure-eight plait on her nape, neat but not exciting. Hagen was used to being with his glamorous wife who had long dark flowing hair and wore the latest and most expensive clothes. Marigold couldn't compete. She could only be herself—a plainly dressed, conservative woman with flyaway hair who would never be anyone else, and possibly by choice. Sometimes she despaired of herself. She could at least decide to adopt Nichole Kidman's precise style.

Hagen's car pulled up outside. She shrugged into her Burberry coat, grabbed up the matching bag, and strode to the door, dressed almost exclusively by Hagen.

"On time," she said, smiling at the best sight she'd seen all day, Hagen wearing dark brown chinos, a beige knit, and a casual coat in tan. "And we match, though that's not too surprising, bearing in mind that I'm wearing your clothes."

"You look better in them than I would." His gaze examined her from her eyes to her feet, and he gave a long slow careful smile. "Did you get your room finished?"

"Pretty well. I have a chair to cover, and it's done. I'm about to start focusing on your house now." That, of course, was a lie, but she didn't want him to know that the minute he'd asked to redo his house that she'd had ideas. She needed him to think that she would spend hours, as many as he'd spent on her house.

"Don't tell me. Show me."

"I wasn't about to tell you," she said, miffed, pulling the door shut behind her. "I'll be spending quite some time on your diagrams, finding you material swatches, carpet colors—"

"I'm allowed to have carpet?"

"I'm not saying. It'll be a surprise."

He ushered her to his car, opening the passenger door. She slid in, worried about the ease with which she had become accustomed to being driven in luxury. He walked around the car and angled in beside her. "Okay, no hints. I love surprises."

"You never used to."

"I do a lot things now I never used to do. You can't expect someone to stay the same all their life. For instance, I'm a little more set in my ways than I used to be."

"That's a sign of age. I'm rather more flexible." She turned her head away.

"Good to hear, Marigold," he said in an impartial voice. "We could possibly now meet in the middle."

Chapter 8

Four o'clock hadn't come fast enough for Hagen. The fear that Marigold's date last night had been successful, that she would continue to see Morgan, set Hagen's teeth on edge. He had waited so long to be with her again and he wouldn't let himself be disqualified before he had fronted up to the starting line.

Unfortunately, although he had been given athletic ability and a certain amount of ambition, he had more idea of how to run a business and organize teams than how to inveigle a woman into his bed. Usually his money did that for him. Begging, of course, was out of the question, except as a last resort. When she had wiped him off her prospective husband list all those years ago, he had not done a single thing about being so summarily dropped, other than to form relationships with the sort of women she expected him to choose. Not that he chose them. He let them choose him.

Marigold had decided that his first chance with her would be his last. She hadn't seen him as steadfast enough to remain by her side while she had gone through the untold torture of caring for the mother she loved. She had an ideal, which he had never managed to fathom. He needed the wholeness she provided that he had never found elsewhere. So, there he sat in a small dark intimate theater, a man with money, no charm, and a yearning for the woman beside him who couldn't be bought.

He shifted slightly to the side and his shoulder touched hers. The contact warmed him. No more than thirty other patrons had decided to see this film and he understood why while he watched beautifully costumed, experienced actors play their roles. Given a choice, he would rather see an art house movie, something dark and complicated, but he enjoyed the comedy of manners well enough. Most of the males in the audience looked as inattentive as he, but for other reasons, possibly.

Hagen's focus was entirely on Marigold, the way the dialogue captured her, the sigh of appreciation she gave with each new scene change. No doubt this stemmed from the designer in her, which he was accustomed to from his sisters, whose recall of movies came from the costumes and the sets. His recall centered on the dialogue. In a careful move, he took Marigold's hand, and she left her fingers in his hold. A good sign? He hoped so.

Finally, the credits rolled and the lights came back on. She turned to him and smiled. "I bet I loved that more than you did."

"I appreciated it, but more than that, I appreciated that you appreciated it. I'm easily pleased. You are not."

"A person tends to get picky when she lives on a limited income."

"Perhaps. I wouldn't know, but I suspect the perfectionist in you is what makes you picky rather than the contents of your purse." He stood. "Let's get you fed."

"You made that sound as though you're not hungry, too."

"My one talent is self-effacement." He gave a deliberately off-kilter grin.

She laughed. "Where are we going?"

"You choose. Do you want to go to a nice little place where we can get a good meal, or do you want to be dazzled by beautiful people spending money?"

"That's a leading question." She followed him down the stairs into the foyer.

"I'm not too subtle, I've been told."

"You clearly want to go to the nice little place."

"I want you to choose."

"You're trying to test me, as usual." She sounded wary as she watched him push open the glass door for her. "What's the prize if I decide to get it right?"

He stood aside holding the door while she walked into the fresh night air. "A nice little meal." A few cars drove past, headlights turned on. The car park in the pub over the road was half-full and the band nothing but a heavy beat as yet.

"I want to be dazzled." With a wholly mischievous smile, she tucked her hand under his arm, watching for his reaction.

He couldn't help smiling back. "No, you don't, unless you've changed quite a lot in the last few years. You dressed to go somewhere quiet."

"So did you."

Covering her hand with his, he moved her in the direction of his car. "So, it's settled. We'll go to the nice little place. By the way, how was your date last night?"

"Oh, dear."

"That good?"

"I'm a dreadful snob. But you know that already."

"What did he do?"

She wrinkled her nose. "Waved his knife around when he talked."

"That was a bullet I dodged." He gave a satisfied smirk.

"Stop pretending that you have no class. You wouldn't wave your knife around because you wouldn't want to take out someone's eye."

He stopped her and examined her face. "You were a snob about me, too, once, but not because of my ignorance of etiquette. You told me I would never amount to much because of my parent's money."

"I used to be perfectly happy to insult you."

"But you're not now?"

"Clearly I've mellowed." She moved so close that her soft hair tickled his face. "But Morgan decided he wasn't as interested in me as he thought he might have been. We had nothing to say to each other. He might have been interested in my contacts, but I think he realized I don't have any."

He studied the expression on her face. "You have a very jaded idea of your attraction."

"I'm realistic. I'll never live in the fast lane he appears to be interested in, the sort you have. I'm a hick at heart."

"I live in the fast lane, do I?"

"Not currently, I suppose, but you'll get back to it."

He had no answer, but he didn't plan on reuniting with his former crowd. They'd been quick with condolences after Mercia's death and equally quick to try to get him back into the social scene. A spare man was always useful and not only for making up the numbers. During the first couple of weeks after Mercia had died, two married friends of hers as well as Scarlett had offered to contribute to his sex life.

Even if he had loved Mercia, the last thing on his mind after she had died so wastefully was sex with one of her hangers-on. He had to go through shock, disbelief, disbelief again, disillusion, and guilt. Always the guilt. If he had loved her, perhaps she wouldn't have died. He had taken quite a while to forgive himself, and he wasn't sure he had, even now.

He opened the passenger door for Marigold, and she slid into the car, folding in her long shapely legs. After carefully shutting the door, he walked around to his side and drove off to his favorite place in Mitcham, a discreet and small restaurant that he assumed Marigold would like. They were seated quickly near the front window in the dimly lit room and the orders were taken. Other people's conversations murmured in the background.

Cutlery clanked discreetly, and the nearby food emitted a delicious aroma. A bottle of red wine was delivered to the table, and two glasses poured.

"This is very relaxing. Good choice." Marigold leaned back, narrowing her eyes with appreciation as she sipped her drink. "Mm. Nice."

"So Morgan didn't get lucky?" He knew he shouldn't ask this and he tensed, waiting for her to tell him her sex life was none of his business, which it wasn't. But if she'd had relations with Morgan, she wouldn't swap over to Hagen, not until the other man was out of her system, so to speak.

She made a rueful mouth. "He wouldn't have called falling into bed with me, lucky. Aside from that, he didn't smell right."

He blinked. "Smell right? He had body odor?"

"No, he's perfectly clean." She shrugged. "I don't know what I mean but when I was close to him, he smelled like a stranger. He didn't have a familiar smell. Normally that would be a compliment, and I don't mean it as an insult but as an observation."

"I have to presume I smell familiar."

"Hah."

"What's that supposed to mean?"

"You're not leading me into any of your traps."

He leaned back, his gaze on her lovely familiar face. "I know what Morgan Evans smells like—books," he said, aiming a satisfied glance at her. "His desk. Chalk. A musty tweed jacket."

She shrugged. "That's the problem when you date strangers. You have to get used to them."

Before he could tell her she shouldn't date strangers, the entrées arrived, a mushroom risotto for him and a prawn salad for her. Yet another lucky save because he knew how she reacted when he told her what to do, or in this case, what not to do. As he ate his main course, a perfectly pink steak, he plotted how to get into her house with her. Most likely she would try to leave him at the door, but if he was ever about to have his second chance with her, he needed his first, the second time around.

She knew his obscure smell, so that wouldn't cut him out of contention, but Hagen didn't want to wait forever for Marigold. If he could bed her, she wouldn't have the bad taste to go out with another man to check his smell.

His tactics planned in his mind, he finished off his second glass of wine. Fortunately, Marigold drank two as well. This would possibly relax the wary creature. "Are we having dessert?" she asked, fiddling with the stem of her wineglass.

"If you want dessert."

"I would like you to have the chocolate soufflé, and I would like a spoonful."

"You can have a whole one of your own."

"I knew you would say that, and you probably know that I won't have one because I'm not hungry. I can only eat a mouthful, and I'm not about to either waste the money or send more food to waste."

He sighed, but only because he would be spending more time in the restaurant and less time in a more intimate situation, with luck. Other than that, her thought processes entertained him. "I'll order whatever you like." He caught the eye of the waitress and within a few minutes, a dessert he didn't want was sitting in front of him with two spoons.

Marigold took the first spoonful. Her eyes closed with sensuous enjoyment. He couldn't remove his gaze for a moment because he imagined that same expression on her face when he made love to her. Although he didn't want the dessert, he ate half anyway because she wouldn't eat more. That was the way she was, controlled in her appetites. Annoying as all hell when he wanted her wild for him. But she never had been. He'd been the one who had always wanted more: more of her time, her attention, and lately her regard. She could pick him up and put him down at will.

He had to force himself to ask her if she wanted coffee. She did. The longer she lingered, the more confidence he lost. She wasn't making any attempt to flirt. She avoided his gaze instead. The time wasn't right. He should forget all about trying for a new relationship with her.

When she finally indicated she was ready to leave, he hustled her out to the car. Once in, she began to make good-bye speeches. He gritted his teeth. "Yes, the meal was good. That's why I like the place. Nothing is too fancy and yet nothing is ordinary. They mix tastes and textures in an interesting way."

"I don't know why you sound annoyed about it. It's a lovely place, and I'm really glad you shared it with me."

"I'm not annoyed," he said, annoyed.

She rested her hand on his thigh, very briefly, as if placating him. "We're nearly home, and really, this has been one of the nicest days I've had in a long time."

He forced himself to relax. "Though, last weekend was pretty good, or that's what I thought you thought."

"It would be hard not to have enjoyed last weekend, or at least for me. I never imagined that I would get my new bedroom done in almost a single weekend."

"You should think about what you're going to do with the sitting room."

"How rude." She sounded prissy but when he turned to glance at her, he noted the upward tilt of her lips.

"You can't say that room is comfortable," he said, frowning at the windshield. "You don't have a chair worth sitting on."

"You didn't do much sitting while you were there."

"You can't depend on all your visitors helping you to paint." He made a right turn onto Kensington Road. The sky was dotted with stars, not the millions a person could see out in the countryside, but quite a few because of the lack of cloud coverage. The temperature outside had lowered a good ten degrees while they'd been in the restaurant.

"It was wonderful what you did, not only the painting, but asking Kell to help as well. I never would have."

"He and Calli have been friends of yours for a while, though. They would have helped at any time."

"I didn't have any work to do because...you know." She glanced away.

"Money. Well, you have a good job, and you'll be able to improve your house little by little." If he thought she would let him, he would drop a bundle of money in her lap right now, or arrange to have whatever she wanted delivered. Better, he would move her into his house where she could have everything her heart desired.

Except, all trace of Mercia needed to be removed from his house before he could offer that and his complete attention to Marigold. He wouldn't normally see himself as a man with little confidence, but since he had been pushed out of contention once with Marigold, the idea of competing with other men tensed muscles in his back that he didn't know he had.

He pulled the car up at the front of her house, noting she'd left the porch light on. "Are you going to let me see your new bedroom?"

She gave him an unreadable glance. "If you are interested, certainly. I would be pleased to do so, but the bedroom itself is neat and new, nothing really unusual."

"Don't be modest. With your taste, it would be quite special." He opened the car door and rounded the front to open her side, too. Unlike most other women, she waited. She expected courtesy from a man, and he imagined she would more often than not be treated like a lady.

"It's nice to have a boss who has faith in you," she said as he handed her out of the low-slung vehicle.

"I believe I'm the first boss you've had." He followed her up the short front path past the fresh spring growth in her garden to the doorway.

She pushed the key into the lock and swung open the door. "I've had a lot of firsts with you." Without giving him any sort of significant glance, she switched on the passage light.

As he had noted before, her house was awkwardly configured. Perhaps the design was smart once, but the whole place needed an overhaul. He would probably shift the bedrooms and bathroom to the front and make an open space of the other rooms. Marigold, on a single wage, would not be able to afford that.

"So, this is my new bedroom." She opened the door and walked inside the room, hooking her handbag onto the door handle.

He followed. "It looks very comfortable," he said, not surprised. "Did you make the headboard?"

Her eyebrows lifted. "Does it look amateur?"

"Not at all. It's perfectly coordinated which means it had to be especially made for the room." He had expected generic modern. Instead he saw a sparsely furnished area featuring a bed with a turned back old-fashioned quilt on the big bed, and a light aqua buttoned headboard of a moderate height. She had only used a few cushions, but to maximum effect. "I wouldn't mind sleeping here myself."

"Make me an offer."

"All my worldly goods," he said caught off guard. He tensed his shoulders and stared at her.

Her eyes glistened, and she stared at him for a few seconds before looking away. "This past year has been ghastly, living alone, seeing almost no one, going almost nowhere. My days used to be filled either with rushing my mother off to the hospital and watching over her while she was there. Or she would be home, and I could cook for her and make her comfortable." Her voice trembled. "Now I go to work and come home to cook for myself. I'm tired. So tired. I need to be held."

He reached out to her and enfolded her in his arms, resting his cheek on her soft hair. "I understand," he said softly, and of course he did. He understood loneliness and regrets as well as anyone. He understood the need to be held, those rare moments of human kindness that so few people could offer. Most people found death awkward and a subject to avoid in conversation. For a moment he stood completely still, appreciating Marigold's warmth and her ability to give as much or more than she received.

As for him, without Mercia's presence, his house was empty. The plain cold white of the rooms added nothing to his life. This room of Marigold's held memories and love. Without thinking about rejection, he stared at her upturned face and slowly lowered his mouth to hers.

The first soft touch of her lips sent his pulse racing. He realized what she meant about smell because hers was sugary and clean, lightly perfumed and warm.

He remembered being twenty and kissing her for the first time at his parent's twenty-fifth anniversary celebration dinner. He hadn't realized how long Marigold had fascinated him but he still had the idea that she judged him and found him wanting. The wanting part was right. He had certainly been aroused, but he had made no further move because his mother had him in her vision.

"Do you remember my parent's twenty-fifth anniversary?" he asked, burying his face in her glorious hair.

She lifted her arms to his shoulders and crossed them behind. "You kissed me." Her body stretched to fit with his. A desire that grew each time he was with her brought his whole body to attention. He shifted his mouth to begin a new kiss while his hands slipped beneath her coat, palming her curvaceous behind. His rock-hard erection settled against her belly. While keeping her gaze on his, she leaned back, smoothing his hair. "Your intentions were as obvious that day as they are now."

He cleared his throat. "Conditioned response."

"Another man would say that I'm irresistible."

"I would rather show you." He put a palm either side of her face and slowly settled his mouth on hers again. As she kissed him this time, her hands clutched his shoulders. She slowly lifted to her toes so that he could let his erection nudge between her legs. His breath shortened. He shifted his hands back to her behind and held her in place, while her forced breathing demonstrated her interest in proceeding.

She began to move, backing toward the bed. "Did you expect this?" she asked, her breath whispering across his lips.

"I hoped," he said into her hair. A half step and he could tumble her onto the bed. He shrugged out of his coat, tossing it over to the chair.

Her coat followed and then she stopped. "So, you've come prepared?"

Caught off guard, he stared at her for a moment. Whether having condoms in his wallet would make him smart or overconfident, he didn't know. "Emergency supplies. I'm an optimist."

"Thank God." And she laughed. "I bought some, too, just in case I could inveigle you into my bed."

He laughed and planted another kiss on her mouth, gripping her waist so that he could lift her onto the mattress.

"Are you in a great hurry to get home?" She dropped with a bounce.

He landed on top of her. "Not at all. I'm hoping to stay the night."

She pushed at his shoulders and shifted her legs out from under him, lifting a knee either side of his hips. "This doesn't feel right."

"It feels good to me." Hard against her tightly covered pubis, he shifted sideways and fumbled for her zipper. "Though I have to admit that it used to be easier in the olden days when women wore skirts," he said, smiling against the side of her neck. He pressed a lingering kiss near her pulse, savoring the softness of her skin.

"It feels planned, emotionless."

Raising his head, he examined her expression, slowly realizing that he couldn't simply pick up where he had left off all those years ago. He needed to spend more time loving her than getting her clothes off. "Marigold, my bright and beautiful flower," he said, gentling his voice. "What I hope is about to happen is far from emotionless, and if this had been planned one of us might have closed the blind." He gently ran his knuckle along the side of her face while he stared into her worried eyes. "I will do that now."

With more reluctance than he could have imagined, he lifted off her and walked over to the window, shutting out any curious neighbors. Then, with forced composure, he sat on the windowsill staring back at her. "There's no hurry, except in my head. If you've changed your mind, I will leave."

"No, Hagen, don't leave. Take off your clothes."

"What, stand here and strip?" Surprised into a smile, he stood, about to do as she requested. Although, even as little as a few weeks ago, he had not expected to have another opportunity with her, getting naked with Marigold had been first on his wish list for many years. "I will if you do."

"You first. One article for you, and then one for me. I'll start." Her brandy-colored eyes large and bright, she sat herself up, removed a shoe, and dropped it onto the floor.

Challenging her with his gaze, he took off one of his shoes, and she scooped off her second. His second went the way of the first. She removed a hairpin. He sat on the side of her bed and removed two socks hoping she hadn't noticed he was in rather more of a hurry than she. Apparently she didn't because she removed her top, leaving her with a pretty blue camisole over her bra.

"I'm calculating who will finish first," he said in a carefully cool voice. "How many hair clips are you wearing?"

She offered a smug smile. "As many as I need to finish after you."

"Thought so." Narrowing his eyes with mock calculation, he pulled his knit over his head, tossing the garment toward the chair. Landing on her coat, his sweater slid to the floor.

She began unzipping her pants.

He watched, knowing at this stage she was in competitive mode and now probably wouldn't change her mind. "Let me help," he said smoothly, glancing at her tiny blue undies beneath and her flat white belly above.

"Ever the gentleman." She lifted her hips to let him scoop her pants down to her ankles, where he left them while he kissed her on the soft flesh just above her undies.

"No distractions," she said, squirming. "I know your tricky little mind."

"I know your tricky little plan. You get me naked and then you have your way with me. You need to lose the idea that I'm easy, woman."

"Hah. You'll be putty in my hands."

"If I am, I'll be very surprised and I hope that you would be, too." Sitting back, he swooped off his white T-shirt, his breath much shorter than he would have liked.

She stopped moving and glanced at his chest. "Do you still swim?"

"Not often. Maybe once a week. How about you?" Although she hadn't backed out, she seemed nervous.

"No. Though I might take it up again if I thought it would put me in as good a shape as you are."

"I doubt anyone would complain about your shape," he said with a heartfelt smile. "You're as toned now as you ever were. What shall I take off next?"

"Your choice, but I think it would be easier to remove your underpants if you took off your trousers first."

He rose to his feet to open his zipper. "I would have both off in a flash if your top was off."

"Do you want me to undress you?"

"Hell, yes." He remembered the condoms, and he tossed his wallet onto her lamp table beside the bed. She had neither grabbed him nor held him off. Puzzled, and growing more uncertain by the second, he turned on the lamp and stepped to the doorway to turn off the main light.

While his back was turned, she had kicked off her pants and had scooted to the top of the bed to shove the bedclothes down to the bottom. "You don't have to completely undress. I don't mind snuggling for a while."

"Good." Diving onto the bed, he scooped her up into his arms. "This is better." He breathed in the closeness of her and the warmth of her body next to his. Only then did he realize that the room had cooled with the night. Likely until then, his hopes had kept him warm. Now with her lovely body in his arms, he reached for the bedcovers to pull over them.

He wrapped her tightly in his embrace and kissed her again. Her mouth met his with a strange shyness, given that they lay entwined, almost naked in her bed. Leaning back, she began a slow exploration of the bones of his face with her palms, smoothing her thumbs across his cheekbones, his eyebrows. Her fingers splayed in his hair.

Not quite so tender as she, he pushed his hands under the back of her undies, enjoying the smooth handfuls of flesh he found, while kissing any of her fingers that came close to his mouth. Then her hands shifted to his shoulders and around his back. When her fingers slid beneath his trousers to his behind, he lifted her closer, remembering she needed to be held. He would have her as soon she indicated she wanted him inside her. Her explorations became torture when she investigated his erection, though he decided a gentleman would make that easier for her.

Momentarily taking his hands from her hips, he slid off his trousers and underpants in one move, leaving himself entirely naked. He kicked his clothes out of the bed. "Let's get you naked, too," he said, finding the lower hem of her camisole.

She sat up. "I'm supposed to be undressing myself."

"Go ahead." His voice came out soft and husky, and he watched her pull her camisole over her head.

She then removed her bra. Her pale nipples, a shade or two darker than her white skin, fascinated him. His own skin had a tendency to tan, despite him having blue eyes and blond hair. Then again, he had Greek and Danish genes. As far as he knew, she was purely British like so many others in Australia.

The side curtains at her window began to stir and rain pattered on the glass. She gave a deliberate shiver and slid back down beside him. He deduced from her movements that she was removing her undies, and oh Lord, he could have her. He groped behind him for the condoms, grabbing his wallet.

Using a single hand and a whole lot of motivation, he slid one out. His wallet dropped onto his shoulder but he held the condom aloft. He put that between his teeth while she laughed.

"Let me help," she said, and she tossed the wallet behind him.

He thought she would take the condom and cover his ready arousal but instead she snuggled onto his chest. Left with the prophylactic, he pushed it beneath the pillow and held her close. With his hands splayed on her back, he kissed her lovely face all over. She kissed him too and suddenly his heart ached. Life was supposed to be like this, full of kisses and warmth. Experimenting with new positions or new partners seemed purely clinical compared to having Marigold in his arms.

When his hands shifted to her breasts, she lengthened against him, her nipples hard and tight. Her legs opened, and she wriggled his aching dick between. By now his need was desperate. He rolled on top of her, and found the hard nub of her clitoris. She bucked. Moving his mouth to her neck, he kissed his way to her lips, sliding his finger along the wetness of her vulva to the entrance of her vagina. She seemed ready for him so he reached for the condom.

Chapter 9

The thought of Hagen's previous experiences intimidated Marigold. If she could control her nervousness, he would never know that she was an elderly virgin. He'd had other lovers. Everyone knew about him and Dido at school, and his sisters had commented on his sex life even before he had married Mercia. He was more experienced than she. She'd only had her dreams.

If she didn't show confidence, he might guess. She hauled in a breath and tried to stop clutching him. As soon as her death grip on him relaxed, he leaned back to roll the covering onto what had to be the largest erection in the whole world, though she had never seen another. And she really liked looking at his.

"It's a shame to cover that pretty thing," she said, wishing she had held her tongue, because he looked astonished.

"You don't want to risk anything." His quick stare at her questioned and answered at the same time.

She moistened her lips. "Of course not." So, now he thought she was an irresponsible idiot. "You could have all sorts of diseases for all I know." She tried a spoiled bitch face that turned a bit soft.

"You're right," he answered, and he looked rueful. "But fortunately I had myself tested recently, and I don't. But you shouldn't take any man's word for this, Marigold. You need to protect yourself." He finished rolling on the condom and focused intently on her face.

"And I will." She offered him her biggest smile. "If this turns out to be more than a one-night stand, I'll also do something about contraception."

Looking amused, he smoothed her hair back from her face with the flat of his hand. "Tonight is your audition. For all I know, you might not work out," he said, with a soft kiss across her lips. "I don't know yet."

"Or you might not." Frowning, she lifted a knee and settled one foot on his taut behind.

"There's a thought." He shifted between her legs, settling the line of his penis to connect with her most sensitive parts. "If I keep talking, I might turn out to be impotent. I've heard that happens to a man when he is diverted from his purpose and dragged into a deep conversation while he is lying splat on a woman."

"There's no reason why we can't be friends, though," she said, forcing her words past her constricted throat. Her spine locked as the condom moved against her.

"Friends with benefits?" He turned his head to examine her expression. She unclenched her hands and shifted her palms to his upper back. His slow movements between her legs had turned into a tease. Despite her tension, she had to fight herself not to arch into him. Trying to remain coolly unsurprised, rather than unbearably excited by the hard thrill of his sliding, she swallowed to moisten her throat. "I suppose that's what we're working up to."

"At this stage of my lack of impotence, I'll take any relationship you're offering." His breath stirred her hair.

She squeezed her eyes shut. "Hug me, Hagen. I'm nervous."

"You're not the only one." He moved his hands beneath her buttocks, cupped, and settled his lips on hers. His mouth opened over hers. His tongue tickled at her lips.

Her hands moved from his wide back and down the sides of his ribcage to his narrow waist. She crossed her legs behind him, her hips tilting and her lower body wriggling until she had the tip of his pressure in place.

For a moment, he let her and then he shifted slightly to put his hand between them. His knowing fingers again found the place that shot a thrill of excitement through her, the clitoris that she'd found some years ago. He continued kissing her mouth, softly, tenderly, and his fingers treated her the same way, with delicate manipulation until she reacted with a hot flow. Then he found entrance, slowly advanced and retreated, pushing through all her years of abstinence.

She remained frozen in place, trying to ignore the sharp pain. When he filled her to the hilt, he stopped moving, which helped a little. He lifted to the full extent of his arms and gazed at her. Her eyes had leaked a little and the tears had flowed into her hair. Fortunately, he didn't appear to notice. His face held an expression she read as a mixture of desire and apology, almost asking for permission too late.

She drew a deep breath and smiled. "You're past the point of no return."

He said nothing. Instead he gave an unreadable smile and began to thrust rhythmically, harder, and if possible, deeper, until she shuddered with each stroke. Finally, she hit the peak she had never reached before. A gush of moisture she couldn't control caused him to utter a sound of wonder, not a known word, simply a sound. She wound her legs tightly around him, and he shuddered, too. Her insides sensitized, she experienced the final jerking of his penis inside her. Then he kissed her face, aiming for her eyes, her nose, and her mouth.

He only said one word. "Marigold." Softly.

Although she'd done almost nothing physical, exhaustion overcame her. She flopped, her hands limp on his back. He settled his weight on her, and she didn't mind a bit. She awoke to find herself snuggled into his arms. Morning light glowed through the sides of the blind.

She focused on Hagen's sleeping face, all hard planes and angles, softened by his thick brown eyelashes. His pale hair sat almost perfectly in place and his bright morning stubble glistened on his cheeks. A welling of love filled her. She wanted him with her every night of her life. For six years she had yearned for this moment, which by rights should never have come.

Mercia should be with him, undeserving, hard, ambitious Mercia who hadn't minded who she walked over to gain the man she wanted. Mercia had been his perfect partner, beautiful, wealthy, and surrounded by admirers who hadn't been able to get enough of her. Marigold could never be Mercia. She didn't have the glamour, the charm, the push and shove.

However, she could have Hagen while he was at a loss, wondering where he ought to go and who he should take with him, if anyone. Marigold's practical self saw that, and her normal responsible self tried not to care. She pondered waking him, but she loved watching his face in relaxation. As she wondered what he might like for breakfast, he awoke. His eyes opened and fixed on her.

"Good audition," he said in a morning fuggy voice. "You got the part."

"How long is the season?" She pushed her fingers through her hair, trying to tidy herself for his view.

"That's up for negotiation. But all the other applicants have been told the role is filled."

"So, breakfast?"

"Let's go out." He rolled onto his back and stretched his beautiful body one long limb at a time, first each arm and then each leg. The man had class. He watched his diet and he exercised and he had the body of a Norse god.

"Where do you swim?"

"At home. I have a lap pool." His expression looked relaxed. "Do you want to try it out later?"

"Is it heated?"

"Give me a break. Who would be motivated to swim in winter if the pool was heated?"

"Me?"

"When did you turn into a wimp?"

"Wasn't I always?"

"Not as far as I recall. You held the school record for 200 meters for two years."

"Someone beat my time?"

"It had to happen eventually."

"I'm not a junior any longer, either. Okay, if I can brave the cold, I'll see how I do in your lap pool."

"That's a date." He kissed her. "While you're drying off after your swim you can walk through my house and tell me what you plan to change."

She snuggled closer. Apparently she would be spending the whole day with him. Then he kissed her again.

An hour later, after he had shown her exactly how he liked to wear a condom, she showered and dressed for breakfast, a sated but apprehensive woman. The only other time she'd been naked with him, she had expected him to blame her momentary lapse on the champagne served at the twins' twenty-first birthday party. She had never expected him to want an explanation, one she wouldn't give, as to why she wouldn't go through what would have been a purely one-night stand. She had put that down to male ego. Without a doubt, she knew he would find a more suitable match than she among one of the many beautiful women in his crowd. And he had.

This time the ending wouldn't be any happier than the last time, although the reason had changed. This time, although she wasn't otherwise obligated, she knew he was. He had the sort of life she wouldn't fit into with the smart, rich people who had scorned her before, who had noticed her cheap clothes and her make-do accessories.

* * * *

Deciding not to care for the time being, she enjoyed a beautifully cooked breakfast with him in a small restaurant in the foothills. After he drove her back to his house, she then enjoyed exhausting herself in his lap pool. She had missed swimming.

Sadly out of condition, she finished her final lap and dragged herself onto the step-out, where she sat with water trickling from the end of her nose. Although she had knotted her hair out of the way, orange clumps clung to her shoulders.

Hagen didn't seem to mind her bedraggled state, though he looked as good wet as he did dry. The sun shone on his golden skin although the October day was cool, and he smiled indulgently at her as, barefooted, he stalked over the paving to the edge of the lap pool, constructed adjacent to the side section of the main heated pool.

"Warm enough?"

"Warm with exercise. Is that towel for me?"

He held out his hand to her, pulled her to a standing position, and he covered her, wrapping her in a thick, luxurious towel and his arms. She snuggled right into him, appreciating his body warmth. He hadn't yet dressed after doing his laps, and he wore racing shorts. His body part pressed against her belly. "Oh, my."

He laughed. "See what you've done to me. Turned me into a randy teenager overnight."

She lifted her face for a kiss. "See what you've done to me. Turned me into a sex-starved spinster."

He kissed her again. He had hurried her through a tour of all the rooms in his house so that they could swim before the predicted rain started, dopey really, when they would get wet either way. The rain hadn't eventuated.

"Come inside, spinster, and get dressed. And then you can tell me what you think I ought to do with the house."

She nodded. "Swimming has relaxed my brain. The ideas are bound to flow."

Using the downstairs bathroom, she showered while he showered and shaved upstairs. He met her in the breakfast room off the kitchen, where she had decided to linger for a view of the lovely garden.

She turned when she heard him behind her. "I'm wondering how attached you are to your white furniture?"

He pulled out a chair at the table for her. "Not at all. Mercia chose it." Whenever he said Mercia, his face closed off.

She understood that he loved and missed his wife and that she would only be a comfortable substitute sex partner, but after all that had happened last night and this morning she didn't want to be reminded. "Well, starting on the hall—I think you ought to keep the marble tiling. This house had marble floors there originally because the hall used to be used as a reception room when the Reynolds had balls. Color on the walls would warm the area, and rugs on the floor. I love the Persian rugs you have in your study. That sort of thing would be nice. And a few paintings."

He nodded. "What do you think of the study?"

"I think it's perfect. I wouldn't change anything there. In the rest of the house, you have a lot of white furniture. It's lovely, but your idea of adding a few antiques would make the house look more relaxed." She looked away, not wanting to criticize Mercia's taste, but Hagen had asked for a change and a change he would have with Marigold's input or without.

"What about my bedroom?"

"The same. We could go to auctions to choose the furniture. Or save time rather than money and use an antique dealer. If you get rid of some of the white furniture, what do you plan to do with it?"

He shrugged. "Donate it to charity."

"What about Mercia's family? Would they like keepsakes?"

"I hadn't thought of that. Good idea. I could ring around and find out." Keeping his gaze on hers, he dragged his phone out of his pocket. "I have her parents' number—and her brother's number."

"You don't waste time, do you, when you have a plan?"

He offered a lazy grin. "No. My motto is do it now. Good morning, Eddie, Hagen here. Yes, yes, I'm well. I was wondering if you or any other member of your family would like something to remember Mercia?"

He listened. "I was thinking furniture. The white pieces."

He nodded. "I remembered you liked the dining room, the table and chairs, the dresser. If you come and get them, they're yours."

He glanced at Marigold. "No. I think her things should go to her family, the cabinets, the hall table, the chandeliers, mirrors. Her bed. Whatever you like. Could you do me a favor and arrange this with the rest of your family?"

He stared at his fingers on the table. "I'm sure you understand why I don't think I should keep her furniture, Eddie." He sounded stiff. Eddie spoke. Hagen moistened his lips. "It's only right."

He nodded again. "Let me know, Eddie. Bye. Done," he said to Marigold. He threaded his fingers together across his upper chest and leaned back in the chair. "Do you want to do a little antique shopping after lunch?"

She glanced at him, surprised. "*Do it now*," she quoted. "Do they want everything?"

"They'll take everything and work out what to do with it."

"You made it sound as if it's their duty to take it."

"Well done, me. Look, if I had sent it to a charity, they never would have known. If they know a worthy cause or if they want it, it lets me off the hook." He sounded hard, and she wondered about his relationship with his wife's family.

"Don't you like them?"

"They're good people but not my relations any longer."

Which told her nothing at all. "So, lunch. Do you have any food here?"

"Nothing much. Imelda caters for me on weekdays, and I buy food or go out on weekends. I'll buy a couple of sandwiches and then we can spend more time shopping."

After confronting his choice of expensively filled wholemeal sandwiches, and eating her fair share, she drove off with him to Magill Road, where antiques and secondhand furniture mingled with coffee and cake shops. In the first place they tried, she spotted an ornately carved mahogany credenza with a white marble top. "What do you think of this for the hall? It would match the floor."

He shrugged. "Do you like it?"

"I like the color of the wood, and having a marble top is a good idea if you plan to decorate with vases of flowers. No water stains to worry about. But it's up to you."

"I plan to decorate with flowers." He grinned. "Probably. I'll get this, and we'll move on."

Farther down Magill Road in a larger antique shop, she found a mahogany dining table with two extensions. "This seats ten without the extensions and twenty with them."

Hagen bought it. "What about chairs?" he asked the dealer.

"I could find something for you," the dealer said, trying to look casual. Marigold assumed he already knew where, and he was mentally assessing the highest price he thought Hagen might be convinced to pay.

"I think it might be an idea to check out modern chairs first." Marigold tried to sound apologetic. Although she didn't want to burst the dealer's money bubble, older chairs were often too uncomfortable to sit in for extended periods and with the entertaining Hagen did, he had to see to the needs of his guests first. Plus, she liked the look of old with new.

Hagen left both options open, disappointing no one. After exhaustive searches in every other possible shop on the strip for antique beds, Marigold chewed on her thumbnail. "There's a shop on Unley Road that lets me borrow furniture for the houses I prepare for sale. His stuff is half trash, half treasure. We probably won't find anything there expensive enough to suit you, but do you want to look anyway?"

"I'm known as a spendthrift, am I?" He raised his eyebrows.

"I have never listened to gossip about you," she answered in a superior voice. As a matter of fact, she had rarely been offered any gossip about him; only snippets about Mercia. "But I've judged you recently and seen that you are not afraid to spend. You buy lunch when you could make it and the same with breakfast."

"Do you want me to save money?"

"What you do with your money is none of my business except when you ask me what you should buy."

"How novel," he said, but when she glanced at him, he didn't look at all supercilious. Instead, he looked indulgent. He pushed his hands into his pockets and raised his eyebrows at her.

Mentally shrugging, she slid into his car again, realizing the dreadful snob inside her loved being in his luxurious car. The dreadful snob also loved stepping out of the car in front of the enormous warehouse full of all the auction rejects.

Bill, the tall, slim, musty owner of the shop offered her one of his shy smiles. Although an astute businessman, he had a kind heart hidden under his unassuming manner. "Another house to do?" he asked her, lifting his shaggy gray eyebrows.

"Today I'm with a bona fide buyer, Bill. This is my friend Hagen. Hagen, Bill Evans."

Hagen shook the older man's hand. "You have set me up for hours of exploration time in here, Bill."

Bill's eyelids crinkled. "You won't see everything in one trip, that's for sure."

"I've never made it to the end of the space, either," Marigold said, laughing up at Hagen. "You could start at one end, and I'll start at the other. I'll meet you in the middle."

Hagen nodded and began to walk to the far end. That's the sort of man he was, methodical. She started at the beginning. That's the sort of woman she was. Hopeful. She found a couple of bedside cabinets that she pulled out for Hagen to inspect. Antique bedside cabinets didn't exist. Commodes were commonly used and some people repurposed them, but this pair had been quality carved from mahogany; modern replicas in bad condition. While she mentally contemplated a re-polish, Hagen loomed beside her. "I've found a treasure." He looked smug.

"Oh, what?"

"A headboard I think will be perfect."

"First look at these bedside cabinets. Polished up, they would look special. What do you think?"

"We'll get them polished."

She liked hearing him say we. "Let's have a look at your headboard."
She followed him to the back of the shop, evading strings of dusty cobwebs.

He had dragged out an enormous slab of carved wood, clearly not an
old English antique. "This looks rather exotic," she said disappointed.

"That's the word, either that or erotic. Look at the carvings."

She peered and saw figures carved in the wood and a closer look revealed
nakedness and group sex involving enormous phalluses and animals. "Don't
tell me you like that," she said, half-shocked. She splayed her hand on the
top of her chest, in a mercy-me gesture.

"I like it, yes. If it's in my bedroom, it won't be on display. I want it."

She lifted her eyebrows. "It might be an antique, but I doubt it has any
value other than as a curiosity."

He shrugged. "It called to me."

"It did not."

He grinned. "Where would I find anything else like this?"

She crossed her arms. "In a brothel. That's probably where it came from."

Hagen stood his ground. Forced to relent, Marigold led the way to Bill's
porcelain crowded sanctuary at the front of the shop. She could barely
look him in the eye when she told him that Hagen wanted the headboard.

"Where did you find it?" She tried to look purely professional.

"That carving has a story. A few years back, one of the old shops in
Rundle Street underwent a restoration. They found this in the roof space.
I reckon someone hid it. Those Victorians were mighty staid. The rest
of the four-poster was rotten. I got this pretty cheap. Quite a bit of it is
sandalwood. Like it, do you, Marigold?"

She glanced at Hagen who seemed to be staring off into the distance.
"Help me here," she said to him.

"She loves it." He slung an arm around her shoulders, drew her to him,
and kissed her forehead. "I wouldn't normally look at anything so shocking
but how could I resist her blandishments."

She sighed. "We've known each other since school days," she said to Bill.

"That explains it." Bill gave one of his long slow smiles. "Want the
bedside tables, too?"

Marigold nodded.

"Four-hundred dollars for the lot?" Bill raised his eyebrows in question.

"Feel free to spend my limited income any way you see fit, Marigold."
Hagen used a long-suffering voice.

She sent him a glance of reproof. "Four hundred it is." She shook Bill's
hand. "Plus fifty dollars for delivery. Pass over your credit card, Hagen,

and write down your address." When she left the shop with Hagen, she said, "You're right. We ought to have a budget. I can order a bed base for you tomorrow. What size do you want?"

"King size, what else? Mercia's brother will have the white one removed tomorrow. I can be set up, minus the bed cabinets, by Tuesday." He sounded pleased. "How long will it take to have the cabinets polished?"

"A couple of weeks, I would guess, at best."

"I'll use lamp tables in the meantime. I'll take them out of one of the guest bedrooms. I think I can get the Allbrook painting team on to repainting the bedroom tomorrow. What color?"

"What color do you want?"

"I asked first."

She wrinkled up her face, thinking. "A darker shade of gray than your carpet. Everything will match with that. That should give you time to think what accent color you would like."

"Marigold," he said using his patient tone. "I would like anything you would like. Find me something beautiful for a bed cover, and I will be happy. I'm sure I can move the paintings in the house around to fit whatever I end up with."

"Right. I'll furnish your bedroom to my taste. So, that's the dining room done except for chairs, and the bedroom done except for accessories. Let me finish off those two rooms before I start on the sitting room. I think your guest bedrooms and bathrooms are lovely already. And I didn't see your bathroom."

"I'll want you in the bedroom by Tuesday night—to see how everything looks." He glanced away as he said the last part.

"Do you expect me to have found your bed coverings by then? I can't. I'll be at work. Unless you think I can spend my lunchtime on your extracurricular activities."

"Now, there's a leading statement. I can let you have a long lunch break, and I'll drive you wherever you want to go in the interests of my bedroom."

Her face began to warm, and she turned away. Although he'd strictly stuck to talking about decorating, her susceptible mind heard that he wanted her in his bedroom by Tuesday night, and she couldn't focus on anything else. The thought of being in his bedroom for purposes other than decorating gave her a full body throb.

While he drove, she stared out the side window of the car, not concentrating on anything but her hopeless yen for Hagen. She had moved out of the one-night-stand category, which was a step up. Last night's audition had earned her the highly desirable job of being his bed partner for the time being. By her reckoning, she would last with him at least until she had finished helping with his house, not that she thought he was fickle, but he clearly wanted to change his bedroom from being Mercia's into his. This hinted at a man with plans to fill the bed with another, or at least rebrand himself for a new relationship.

Marigold wanted to dawdle with the job, but he had hurried her along too well for her liking.

"My bed will be gone tomorrow." He sounded satisfied. "I'm going to need a place to sleep for a while."

"Says the man with three spare bedrooms."

"Let's not ruin a perfectly good weekend by sending me off home on Sunday night."

"Well, let's not pretend you're homeless. Let's pretend you want to be with me."

He pulled the car up outside her house. "Bad move, huh? I wasn't quite sure you wanted to be with me, so I thought the pity card might work."

"If you think I sleep with men because I feel sorry for them, you need to think again. I need to be very attracted to someone before I sleep with him."

"Can I attract you two nights in a row?"

"We'll see."

He drew an extended breath and opened his door. Within moments he had rounded the car and opened her door, taking her hand to help her out. "What do you want to do about dinner? A quick meal at the local?"

* * * *

"Do you see anything you want on the menu board?" Hagen asked as he escorted Marigold to the empty table by the window. He had made a reservation at an Italian restaurant that he had always liked, while she'd changed out of the black pants and top she had been wearing all day, to a black skirt and top. Outside, the daylight had begun to fade.

"I'm going to get fat if we keep eating out. I'll have the marinara."

He paid for two. He had never much cared what he ate, but apparently she did, which worked in his favor since he wanted her to move in with him. If she did, she could get Imelda to prepare anything she wanted. That was the way meals had been organized when Mercia was alive. She had done very little cooking herself, despite her extensive shopping.

Marigold didn't want wine with her meal, and that suited him, too, although he usually had a drink when he ate out, if not half a bottle. As he toyed with his water, he said, "I've heard that if you do the same thing for four days in a row, you're on the way to forming a habit."

"In relation to what?"

"Specifically, in relation to having a drink with a meal, but also for exercise, like taking a walk after dinner. Apparently you can make that into a habit."

"I think I've made reading into a habit." She twirled her spaghetti around her fork. "I always read a few chapters before I go to sleep."

He grinned. She hadn't read a word last night. "Unless you are otherwise occupied."

"Let's rephrase that to say unless I'm distracted." Her lips pressed together as if she was deliberately trying not to smile, but her eyes crinkled slightly. "If you stay with me tonight, what are you going to do in the morning?"

Tricky. "How about what we did this morning?" He tried not to look too keen.

Her cheeks turned pink. "I meant about dressing and going to work."

He considered. "I'll go home and shower and dress and drive off to work as usual."

"We wouldn't want Sandra knowing where you spent the night."

"She thinks I'm celibate."

"And were you?"

He kept his gaze steady. "For some time."

"Everyone has to break out eventually."

"What about you?"

"I'm breaking out with you." She looked away.

Once, he had thought he would never get that chance. Years ago, she had told him in no uncertain terms that his future success was assured because of his parents' hard work and ambition, and not because he was any sort of genius. The harsh assessment had decided him to ask her to waltz with him at the school formal. Her date had left her with egg on her face. Even if she had seen Hagen as nothing but a rich boy, at least he had cared.

In those days, if she had refused to dance with him, he would have had enough front to imply he'd been joking, but back then he had the bolstering of his peers. Now, he was on his own, wanting a woman who had pricked his ego long ago, by being patently uninterested in him. These days, she seemed more likely to accept a relationship.

Bedding her had been a good start, but he wanted more than a quick tumble. Agreeing that she was breaking out with him was a step up from the, "no thanks," he'd heard during his third year at the university when he had yet again tried to get a date with her. He waited for a year before he tried again. The fast-flowing champagne at his parents' party six years ago had caused her to relax. Far from turning her back on him, she had latched onto his arm and said something ridiculous. He had kissed her. More than once. He hadn't wanted to stop. She made him laugh, she made him think, and she stimulated him with her rigid opinions.

He had taken her to a rock concert the next weekend, and the next day to a barbeque that ended late at night, after which he circumspectly took her home. The next weekend they spent together with his friends. By that time, he was dazzled. Her kisses told him she was, too. One thing had led to another and they'd ended up in his university boarding house.

He had half undressed when she'd pushed him away with her polite rejection. And she'd told him that she didn't want to see him again. Clearly his constant presence had begun to bore her to distraction. He saw no point in breaking his heart over a woman who only viewed him through champagne glasses. The confidence he had lost returned—to a degree. In his usual crowd, he was still a catch. So he had moved back with them and tried to forget Marigold, who had apparently forgotten him instantly.

And here she was, the same Marigold who picked and chose whatever and whomever she wanted. Last night had told him that if he had ever been a dud in bed, or if she had ever thought he might be, she didn't now. She had been, as ever, the perfect partner for him. Sex with her last night was real, no deliberate scratching of his skin, none of that biting that was supposed to stimulate him into rough sex. He also wanted loving sex: he wanted to get to know her likes and dislikes.

That night, he discovered that apparently she liked him. When he awoke the next morning, he didn't want to leave the bed, or leave her. She bemused him. She thrilled him. He had never experienced a night like that. Sex made with love was a whole other experience, on his part. He didn't know about her. She had always been a mystery to him.

While she watched with sleepy satisfaction, he dressed and went home for a shower, a shave, and a change of clothes, quite determined to spend every single night in her bed until he could manage to move her into his.

Chapter 10

If there was such a thing as a sex hangover, Marigold was experiencing one. She had overdosed on sex the night before, testing her own limits, until she realized she didn't have a limit. Given the chance to explore Hagen's body, she had touched every inch of his smooth golden skin. Some inches were more impressionable than others, but even kissing his ears stimulated him. She found that endearing, mainly because that had to be an emotional reaction rather than sexual. The thought that he had real feelings for her was a sexual turn on.

She walked into the office in the morning, a more than satisfied woman. Having already spotted Hagen's car outside, she was safe in the knowledge that he had arrived first. She prepared herself to act as she always had when she saw him, hoping she didn't have any sort of smug happiness lurking on her face.

She didn't know how he had managed to coax another two orgasms out of her last night, though he was in superb condition. Largely, and she appreciated the word largely far more now, she'd had little to do with this. She had only needed to relax and appreciate every single one of his sensual explorations.

Trying to blink him out of her mind, she said, "Morning, Sandra."

Sandra raised her head. "Rough weekend?"

"Do I look that bad?" Marigold checked with her hand that her hair was still knotted at her nape.

"I say that to everyone in the hope that someday I'll hear a morsel of interesting gossip."

Marigold stopped. "Do you say that to Hagen?"

Sandra made a rueful face. "Not since Mercia died. Even I have some tact. There are a couple of surprises for you on your desk."

"Good surprises or bad surprises?"

"One of each, I suspect, depending on the way you feel about Hagen."

Feel about Hagen? Marigold didn't answer but she hurried into Tiggy's office with a degree of apprehension. She noted the first surprise straight away—a new cell phone tied with a pink ribbon, accompanied by slip of notepaper. Angling into her chair, she read: *The company phone as promised, darling. Alex put in all the numbers he thinks you will need for the job including mine and his. Enjoy. Demi. Kisses.*

She found the next surprise when she opened a thick white envelope containing an invitation to the company's annual dinner, a formal event for the affiliates, on Wednesday night. For this she would need to be on her best behavior, which wouldn't be a stretch at all. One thing her mother had taught her had been how to behave in any social situation.

Long ago she had discovered etiquette didn't matter as much as her mother supposed, because almost no one else had been schooled the way she had. She knew who should sit with whom and where each person should be seated. She knew the correct placement of every eating implement invented and how to use each one. Proper table settings had been drummed into her head. Even when she wasn't in the security of her own home, she rearranged knives and forks in restaurants before she could eat if they had been incorrectly placed.

Sometimes she thought she should have taken a job as an etiquette adviser.

She even knew how to converse with a bore. Aside from her date with Morgan, the latter skill had never been needed.

"What do you think?" Sandra stood in the doorway.

"About the surprises? Nice phone. Very nice phone."

"What about the invitation? It came from Hagen."

"Also"—Marigold cleared her throat—"very nice."

"It's a big step for him," Sandra said in a serious voice. "Since Mercia passed away, he has gone to these functions without a partner. You must have done well enough at his dinner to have passed his test. He couldn't take any old body. He needs someone who can help him represent the firm."

"That's flattering to know that he thinks I can. So, I'll have to schmooze a few bigwigs, will I?"

Sandra offered a stretched smile. "Mercia used to hate the business dinners. You don't have her temperament. You can do it," she said, nodding. "That's not to say Mercia couldn't." She glanced away.

Marigold didn't want to know what perfect Mercia did or didn't like to do because going to any sort of dinner and finding someone new to talk to was a novelty for her and one she was likely to enjoy very much. "Should I answer this formally?"

Sandra shook her head. "I'll let Hagen know that you would be delighted to join him."

Putting aside her constant problem about having nothing suitable to wear, Marigold grabbed up her new phone and hurried off to the warehouse. Today she would begin the staging of the school duplex. The bathrooms and kitchens had been installed last week and the carpets should be down this morning. Billy and Joe would be loading the truck but she still needed to find vases and table settings.

By the time the truck left, she had organized everything she needed. She followed in her car. First, she helped the men unload and then she directed them as to placement, ducking the carpet men, and making sure not to trip over discarded remnants. She didn't have time to think about Hagen.

By lunch break, the right furniture had been placed in the right rooms in each side of the duplex and the curtains had been hung. "I think I'll be okay from here," she said to Billy. "I won't need to shift anything heavy around. If I need you back, I'll call. I now have a company phone." She waved the latest in a brand of gleaming new technology while she smiled with satisfaction.

The men acknowledged the beauty of her newest acquisition with a grin and finished off the dregs in their cups. "Let Kell know if you want anything else delivered," Billy said, rising to his feet. "He can put the smaller things in his pickup." He swiped up the mess from the table and took the wrapping paper, orange peel, and shards of lettuce with him to dispose of.

Watching him, Marigold appreciated the work ethic of everyone employed by AA & Co. She'd thought she would be glad to leave and go back to her old way of life but after almost a month working outside her home, she had found a real life, one that contained other people and cooperation and daily conversations. How novel, as Hagen might say. And there, far too easily, he had slipped into her thoughts.

Forcing herself not to think about him or last night, she concentrated on the job at hand, which was that of a shelf stacker, though she used more interesting items than cereal boxes. Working on the first house, she finished the bedrooms. In this ex-industrial area, modern generic would suit best, though she retained touches of the school building ethos with the chalkboard panel in the kitchen, an old desk in one of the smaller bedrooms, and a large black-and-white print of the original school in the fifties blown up into an art piece.

She had chosen mid brown for the carpeting and the same shade for the floor tiles in the kitchens and bathrooms. Both these areas in both these houses had been tiled with block white and grouted in a darker shade to match the floors. So far, safe for all tastes. All walls had been painted slightly off white. With the neutral background, she could showcase various colors, giving buyers without their own set opinions options for decorating. White blinds had been hung on every window.

By the time she left at five, she had provided a young child's colorful bedroom, a teenager's moody bedroom, and a glamorous main bedroom. The kitchen, featuring glossy oak cabinets with polished granite countertops, opened into the dining and sitting room, furnished to match with light oak tables and fabrics in subdued blues ranging to cream. The other duplex she would finish with Mercia white and bright colors, but she would do that tomorrow.

Her phone rang while she was hauling herself out of her car in the Allbrook's lot. She glanced at the screen and her heart sang. "Hagen," she said in a husky voice.

"Finished?"

"I'm in the car park now."

"Meet me at my house in an hour." And he rang off.

* * * *

Hagen had never been hopelessly besotted before. He had no doubt everyone would glance at him with amazement if he mentioned that Marigold had turned his life around. Marigold. Perceptive, careful Marigold—a woman without a touch of wildness, a practical woman whose every considered word was a delight to him. Being with her forced him to think about the years of emptiness he had suffered until he had her in his life again.

Marigold was no privileged princess. She was a real woman who spoke her thoughts, but never in a harsh way about others. He doubted she would ever put him through criticisms of his family, and he didn't need to be defensive about who he chose as his friends. She would gather her own as wisely as she had accepted his sisters, and she would consider deeply before she judged a person's actions.

He glanced around his new bedroom, wondering how she would judge him if she knew the truth about his dysfunctional marriage. He had behaved ignobly for too long and she would have expected better of him.

The doorbell rang, and he glanced at his watch. Six. He smiled to himself as he bounded down the stairs. She even had a promptness gene. He doubted she would ever keep him watching the time if he had a deadline to meet. She shared his opinion of people who thought their time more important than the time of others. She would make a call of bad manners, and he agreed. Long ago, he had decided her values were the same as his.

When he opened the door, he let a lazy smile form on his face. "Thank God you were out of the office all day."

"I didn't miss you, either," she said, with mock hauteur.

Swooping her into his arms, he almost swung her across the doorstep and into the house. "Unfortunately, we need two separate lives, one for the office and one for home." He nuzzled his face into her hair while he pushed the door shut with his foot. Her hands settled safely on his chest while his lips found hers.

"Do your comfort women usually run to your call?" she asked politely, when she finally leaned back and smiled into his eyes.

"Only if the call is urgent." He turned, his arm around her shoulders while he walked her to the stairway. The rail had been stripped of the white paint today. Tomorrow the French polishing would begin. "My bedroom is finished except for the look. It's ready to be occupied."

"You don't waste time, do you?"

"Nope. When I have a plan, I execute it as swiftly as I can." He led up the stairs and ushered her into his bedroom.

She stood in the doorway glancing around. "You've had that dreadful headboard attached to the wall. Good idea. It looks very classy from a distance despite the whole disgraceful lot of it showing. Those satyrs around the bottom are having a merry old time."

"You can't see that from here." He frowned.

"I don't have to," she said in a severe voice. "I know they're there. The room smells like new paint."

"I hope that won't put you off."

"It doesn't bother me a bit. I don't have to sleep here."

He moistened his lips. "You don't have to, no. But if I sleep at your house every night, soon enough someone will mention my car outside in the street. Or do you expect me to walk over?"

"Do you want me to sleep here?" She looked astonished.

"You agreed to be my comfort woman. I wouldn't be comfortable without you sleeping with me. I have room for your clothes here and your car can be garaged. And I can make sure you eat properly."

"A self-serving statement if ever I have heard one. I always eat properly. You're the one who eats out all the time."

"Will you, or will you not, share this bedroom with me?" He put his hands on his hips.

"I'll think about it."

Fortunately, he now knew that meant yes. "About dinner. I had a meal for two prepared. Nothing special. Simply good, healthy food. My daily help is intrigued. I wouldn't be surprised if she comes early tomorrow to inspect you."

"You're taking a lot for granted."

He turned into her. "I can't let you out of my life just yet," he said in a low voice. He examined her face, his chest aching with love, hoping he wasn't taking anything for granted, hoping she had the same feelings about him as he had about her. Slightly shaky, he hauled in a breath. "Now, about that corporate dinner. We've invited people who would be useful to us in a business sense. The main guests are the heads of the superannuation funds. We need to pitch to them in terms of the market and investment."

"Your expectations of me are far too high," she said, her expression astonished. "The amount I know about markets and investments is exactly nil."

"You don't need to know anything. You'll be there to make me look good."

"I'm a handbag at my first corporate dinner," she said in a doleful voice. "I never thought I would sink so low."

"I can be yours at an art show." He took her into his arms and leaned back with a grin. "You can't be expected to know my job. I want you there to relax people into thinking I'm an okay guy. Okay guys wouldn't let them down in a business sense."

"I suppose this is the sort of thing partners do for each other." She toyed with the hair on the nape of his neck.

"Exactly." His voice came out satisfied. "And as your partner, I know you will be fussing about what to wear. If you won't wear anything I have hanging in the room that is now your dressing room, or if nothing there suits you, I'll have the lot removed. I'll also give you time off to buy a few formal outfits at the company's expense, of course."

"Do you buy Sandra's clothes?"

"I don't use Sandra as my escort to important dinners. Though, perhaps I should. She would put quite a few people into their proper places. I expect you to charm them so that our company is remembered."

She stared at him for a beat too long. "Leave the clothes. I don't want to be accused of wasting your money. I'll need to move a few other things here, too, but I don't want to move in, not completely."

He whooshed out a breath. His ambit bluff had worked. Even if she stayed over sometimes, he considered that a win. "This is, of course, a sneaky tactic on my part. If you sleep here, you'll hurry up with the plans for rest of the house."

She pushed him away and then grabbed him back and kissed him. He had never had pre-dinner sex in his whole life, and he thought she had somehow brought out the irresponsible teenager in him. He was putty in her hands, except in the one place where she made sure he wasn't.

Finally, after they had eaten, he sat watching the log fire crackling. "This might be our last fire of the year. It wasn't cold enough tonight to have one, but I wanted the coziness."

"There's a designer hidden somewhere in you. You're visualizing the look rather than the practicality. Speaking of which, do you have something for me to wear in bed tonight?"

He stared at her.

"Right," she said, blushing. "I don't know what I could have been thinking."

* * * *

Yet again, Marigold arrived at work after Hagen. Today she had seen him off after being introduced to his daily help, Imelda, a tiny middle-aged woman from the Philippines. Imelda looked her up and down, and didn't seem to approve until she discovered Marigold had agreed to try a couple of the gowns in Hagen's wardrobe. After that, she eyed Marigold speculatively. Perhaps Imelda had met other women who stayed overnight with Hagen and wondered how long Marigold would last.

As she had yesterday, Marigold left the office with the next load of furniture for the second duplex. She left at five after finishing the staging to her satisfaction, rather amazed that she had designed two whole interiors without a glitch. Whether her designs would sell the houses remained to be seen. She didn't have the same natural flair as Tiggy, but she liked both the duplexes herself and found the spaces she had designed livable.

Since no one ever seemed to check up on her, she would have to take full responsibility if she had failed—if anyone even told her she had failed. That might be Hagen's job, which would make matters awkward, since she was sleeping with him. The old adage about not bringing the job home clearly had some disadvantages—for him, rather than her. Well, his job, his problem. If all else failed, he could always ask Tiggy to wave her magic wand, and hey presto, a good sale.

In the evening, she planned to pack her bags for a few days' stay with Hagen. The idea half appalled her and half delighted her. Being with him made her empty life into one of completion. She had never imagined he would forgive her for refusing him all those years ago. He had an ego, like most people.

He had been right about his car in the street outside. For her whole life, she'd had the same neighbors. She doubted anyone would be scandalized by his car being left there overnight, but as soon as he moved on, they would be swift with condolences. All over again she would be poor Marigold. Being lucky Marigold suited her much better. She now fit into the definition of shallow.

She wallowed in the thought of having her meals prepared and someone to clean up after her, and she would manage being treated like a spoiled rich girl as long as she could. Sex once or twice a night wasn't too hard to bear, either. This morning, she had initiated a bout herself. Watching Hagen wash his gorgeous, big body had turned her into a mouth breather, and she had practically tripped herself up in her speed to join him under the shower.

After the second duplex had been furnished with light painted wood to match the creamy-white kitchen, and after green and melon accents had been added, she had raced home and left within fifteen minutes. Hagen was waiting for her in the kitchen. As she walked apprehensively through from the garage, he grabbed her into his arms and kissed her.

"You didn't bring much luggage," he said into her hair.

"Mainly underwear. I sort of wear a uniform to work, in case you hadn't noticed." She leaned back and stared into his warm blue eyes.

A satisfied smile curved his lips. "I didn't. I must have been too busy looking at your breasts."

She placed her hands flat on his chest. "You're never going to shock me because I know you don't do that sort of thing to women."

"Don't be too sure," he said in a drawling, superior voice, deliberately staring at her not particularly lush cleavage. Then he flashed his golden Hagen smile. He passed her a glass of champagne. "This is to celebrate your first official night here. Leave your bag. I'll take it upstairs later. Do you want to eat in the dining room or the morning room?"

"We could try out the new table in the dining room. I saw some chairs today that might be okay in there, too. They have soft brown leather seats and slightly curved legs. I saw them online, so I haven't checked for comfort."

"Would you be willing to sell your dining chairs? You have a set of twelve." She pursed her mouth, thinking. "They're antiques and not very comfortable."

"What about mixing them with the more modern ones? We would have to because you don't have enough for this house."

"I'm sorry, Hagen. I can't. They're from the original settlers in my mother's family, the only thing handed down from them. Her cousins didn't get much, either, but not a lot was left in the end."

"It was just a thought. I'll take a couple of the morning room chairs in there for the time being. Imelda left a curry for tonight. I'll zap it."

She ate with him and after dinner, she took her clothes into her dressing room while he tidied up in the kitchen. While she was there, she skimmed through the racks, wondering what to wear tomorrow night. At least four of Hagen's gowns would qualify as formal. She had her heart set on one. She didn't know how she could have missed seeing it before. The only other time she had been in this room, she had noted the two black formal gowns that would look very smart and the white that wouldn't do a lot for her coloring. The previously unseen yellow would warm her almost blue white skin. And she craved that gown with every little craving gene she had in her body. But would an event coordinator wear a heavy lace gown that everyone would know must have cost a small fortune?

She had no idea.

* * * *

While she showered before changing the next night, Hagen refreshed his shave. "What are you wearing tonight?" he asked, twisting his mouth for a razor stroke along his chin. She loved the way that even the hair on the back of his hands gleamed golden.

"One of your black gowns. That would be more in keeping if I need to stay in the background." She stepped out of the shower, grabbing for the towel. Water dripped from her head.

He eyed her. "What gave you the idea you need to stay in the background? You're my partner for the night."

"I'm representing the firm."

He nodded, evading her gaze in the mirror. "Then, black is a wise choice. We're a flamboyant newly rich family. We ought to be modest about our wealth. Anything less than black would be flashy."

"I, however, am not an Allbrook." Raising her chin, she shot him a challenging glance. "If I want to wear, oh hell, a bright yellow dress, I can."

He stared at his own face in the mirror and wiped the soap from his chin. "I'll stick to black and white."

She wrapped her wet hair in a towel. "Well, should I wear the yellow or not?"

"I bought it for you to wear but if you don't like my taste, I'll return it."

"You bought it?"

He shrugged, half smiling. "Not personally. I described your coloring and the shop's stylist chose it for you."

She moved across the warmed marble tiles to reach his side. "Thank you," she said, her voice husky. "It's beautiful. I've never owned anything as beautiful."

He turned, glanced into her eyes, and cupped one hand beneath her chin so that he could place a careful kiss on her lips. "That's enough of that. We need to arrive there early. I can't have you distracting me." With a wide smile, he left the bathroom to her.

* * * *

Hagen finished dressing in his black suit and knotted his black tie, wondering if he had been out of line buying Marigold's gown. More than likely, she would prefer to choose one herself, but then she would insist on paying. He knew her wage as well as he knew his own, and the two didn't compare. Although she would have looked equally stunning in one of the blacks, he had the idea she ought to stand out from the crowd. If she didn't want to, she'd had the choice.

As he was leaving the bedroom to wait downstairs, she came out of the bathroom, wearing his toweling robe. He made a mental note to buy one for her, too, and he stood breathing in her glamour. "You look good."

"I'm wearing lots of makeup."

"Maybe, but you're a beautiful woman."

She smiled. "Let's hope I don't let you down."

"You couldn't." In the artificial light, her eyes looked like molten gold framed in ebony, mysterious and exciting. Her skin had a pearly sheen. She had straightened her hair and a waterfall of red-gold hung to her shoulders. He had to glance away for a moment to take back control of his feelings for her. In his eyes, no one could be more beautiful or more desirable, but overwhelming her with his needs at this stage would be unwise. First, he wanted to hear she liked more about him than the way he could urge a response to his desire. "I'll wait for you in the living room."

She had always appealed to him physically because of her beautiful toned body, but after he'd gotten to know her, and realized she wasn't a smart arse, he appreciated that she stood out from the crowd because no one ever intimidated her. She had a rare confidence in herself, a maturity that other girls lacked, an independence that he also admired. He should never have let her leave him without a word. He had allowed her to dump him because of his own ego, his refusal to chase her.

If he had tried, despite living in the university college and not at home, he could have had regular news of her from his sisters, with whom he connected in passing. While they were studying, the twins had lived together in one of Far's rentals not too distant for him to visit from time to time. Instead, he had thrown himself into the life of an eligible single—drinking too much, concentrating too little on his studies, and generally being irresponsible. He'd never had a steady girlfriend until Mercia, who hadn't let herself be shaken off. And so he eventually married her, hoping for a marriage like the one his parents had, a union of energetic people with similar goals.

Deciding not to pour a pre-dinner drink, he wandered restlessly around the house, from the pristine kitchen, through the half-renovated dining room, and into the sitting room. He gazed through the French doors at the garden, nothing on his mind but his mistakes. With the chance to begin again, he hoped he wouldn't make another.

As the grandfather clock in the hall chimed the quarter hour, the creak in the staircase warned him Marigold was ready. He turned and realized that he had chosen exactly the right stylist for her. The heavy lace gown covered her from the neck to the calves and the elbows, and clung to her every feminine curve. She had done a Jessica Rabbit style with her hair, one side tucked behind her ear and the other seductively clinging to her cheek. She turned for his inspection. The back dipped low and showed the pristine white of her skin that, against the gold of the gown, looked delicate and somehow pure.

"Very nice." He tried to sound impartial but she was smart enough to read his dazed expression.

"Thank you. It may be gauche to say this, but this is my very first grown-up gown and the very first time in my life I have felt beautiful."

"It's not, however, the very first time you have looked beautiful. You always do." He shrugged, awkward in his praise.

"You look very handsome yourself, but then you always do. Always have."

He noted she wore her pearl earrings, and he approved the simplicity. "We chose our parents wisely."

"Is this bag suitable?" She held a quilted clutch in black to match her shoes.

"I don't know why women have to have bags."

"Because we don't have pockets. I need tissues in case I cry and lipstick in case I eat."

He laughed. "Let's go. If you don't eat, the venue will answer to me."

"Tough guy." She hitched a hand under his arm and walked beside him to his car.

When they arrived at the venue, they weren't the first on the red carpet, which gave him an opportunity to introduce her to the lingering businessmen he knew by name, but first he pulled her up in front of his parents in the foyer.

His mother took her hands and kissed her on the cheek. "You look very intelligent," his mother said to Marigold. "I've been told we are not supposed to tell women they look beautiful because we're affirming that looks are all that count."

Marigold stopped a sudden spurt of laughter. "The smart color of this dress wasn't even my idea. Hagen found a stylist." She lifted her shoulders in a shrug.

"Hagen?" His mother tilted her eyebrows, her face expressing overdone shock.

He found he needed to glance at his shoes. "She hasn't been in the workforce long enough to have an outfit for every occasion. She ought to get a modicum of use out of that one." He kept his voice and his face cool.

"They don't wear those outstanding dresses as often as you might imagine," his father said, seriously. "But, Marigold." He turned to her. "You look very beautiful." He clasped her shoulders and drew her to him in a bear hug.

Marigold leaned back and stared directly into his eyes. "Thanks, Alex. And to be PC, so do you. Demi looks intelligent."

His mother preened, but she always looked smart. They separated, his parents introducing moguls to financiers and vice versa while Hagen concentrated on moving Marigold around the room for maximum exposure to the people he knew.

He spotted Calli and Kell near the entrance, and indicated to Marigold that they would move in that direction. In the middle of the crowd, he got sidelined. Scarlett Haines reached across Marigold and grabbed his arm, leaning forward to press her cheek to his. Apparently, she didn't intend to waste her lipstick so early in the night, and for that he was grateful, but she was effectively standing in front of Marigold and blocking her. "Hagen, darling, meet Mike McManus, my dashing escort for the night."

Hagen turned slightly to the right so that he could use his right arm to grab Marigold's nearest arm from behind. Somehow, he encouraged her to move behind him to his right side. "Delighted," he said to Mike and shaking the hand of a chap in his fifties who stood a head shorter than him.

"His delightful wife thought she could trust him to me tonight." Scarlett gave Hagen the sort of look that said she was warning the other man that he was nothing but a handy date and by no means a person with whom she would pursue an illicit relationship.

"Marigold, you know Scarlett, and Mike is one of our investors." Hagen read that on Mike's name badge.

Marigold offered her hand to Mike and a smile to Scarlett. "How nice to be with a man whose wife trusts him," she said politely. "I don't know how rare that is, but it's nice to hear all the same."

Trust Marigold not to say anything conventional. Hagen grinned at her.

"Good evening, Marigold. Marigold works in Hagen's office," Scarlett said to Mike. "She does all sorts of marvelous things with furniture. And yes, plenty of trusting wives have found out too late about an erring husband playing around and not necessarily with strangers. Sometimes they play around with the wives of best friends."

Hagen's face froze with horror. "Enjoy the dinner." He tried a blank smile. With whatever expression he finally managed, he placed a guiding hand on the back of Marigold's waist and moved her on.

Scarlett's indiscretion would be dealt with later.

Chapter 11

After being introduced to too many people whose names began to interchange, Marigold was finally ushered into the main ballroom of the convention center. Against the black background, the pristine white-clothed round tables gleamed in the dim lighting. Fortunately, enough space had been left between the seats for invitees to push through to their designated tables.

Hagen's was in front and to the right of the shoulder-height podium. Following Calli and Kell, Marigold stopped at her place name. The others moved farther along, past the table that would seat Demi and Alex, the governor of the state and his wife, and various other dignitaries, and to the table on the left.

"Everyone at our table is either a major investor or a prospective one," Hagen said into her ear. "Don't get drunk and don't sit on anyone's lap."

"I'll do my best, though a couple of the bellies over there would make the last fairly difficult."

However, she discovered she wouldn't be seated beside Hagen but almost directly opposite. Two strangers, who would prefer to have the ear of someone influential would have her attention instead. Anyone married to Hagen would be stuck with this sort of placement forever. Lucky her, that she found a plus in never being his wife.

She made sure of memorizing all the names written on the place cards, and saw that Scarlett Haines would also be at Hagen's table, though not next to him either. As everyone seated his or herself, she saw his dinner partners for the night were older, respectable looking women who wouldn't cause Marigold to turn green with jealousy. Unfortunately, Scarlett did. Scarlett effortlessly wore a silver gown with a sequined bodice. She looked like an expensive trophy, in the same way Mercia always had, the perfect corporate wife.

Then Alex Allbrook appeared on the podium and said a few words in his calm way about AA & Co. When he sat again, the meals began to stream out of the kitchens. She liked the man either side of her, but the problem with big dinners was that people couldn't hear anyone farther away. Before the main course arrived, Hagen also spoke to the gathered guests. She had never been so nervous in her entire life, though she knew he was a good speaker. He'd had plenty of practice at school, and likely at the university too.

Thomas on her left whispered, "You must be very proud of your boss."

"Sure am," she whispered back. "This is the best job I've ever had."

After the main course, people began to move around the room to network. Hagen left to speak to his father. She had no networking to do, but remaining seated clearly obligated Thomas to remain, since Bertrand on the other side had left. She wondered if she ought to try a conversation with Scarlett, who apparently had connections useful to Hagen. Plus, her comment about husbands playing around had been rather pointed, and had clearly annoyed Hagen.

She stood, but Scarlett had disappeared. At that moment, Calli touched her shoulder, smiling.

"That gown," she said in a reverent voice. "Gold. Good as gold, Marigold. You rock that color."

"I never would have thought of wearing it. I keep to safe colors as you know, but the moment I saw it, I fell in love. If I spend the rest of my life paying Hagen back for this gown, that wouldn't be too long."

"I've never thought of my brother as a fashionista." Calli laughed. "He has always made it quite clear that he is not interested in colors or styles. But if he expects you to pay him back, I'll certainly have something to say. You can't buy something for someone and then charge them." After her supportive words, Calli tucked her hand under Marigold's arm. "It's noisy in here with all the men gossiping. Come to the loo, and we can gossip in the queue."

Marigold led the way through all the black suits and into the foyer. From there, Calli led the way to the ladies' room. "I've been in this conference center many times before. Ma and Far do one of these big dinners every year. Kell will be speaking before dessert. He's half-annoyed and half-pleased, but Far has been impressed with him from the start and thinks he is a great asset. So do I." Calli deliberately fluttered her eyelashes. "For entirely different reasons."

When Marigold had finished in the loo, she stepped outside to make room for the lines of women waiting to enter. Calli hadn't yet left. Like someone about to cross the road, Marigold looked to the left, looked to the right, and spotted Hagen disappearing around the corner in the direction of the atrium. Since the dinner had begun, she hadn't spoken to him, though she had caught his glance a couple of times. Reining him in now for a comfortable review of the night so far seemed like a good idea.

Clutching her little bag under her arm, she managed a catwalk strut in her heels. Apparently, he hadn't quite reached the atrium because she heard his voice. "I thought we agreed to keep it quiet." His voice sounded deep and cool.

A woman answered him. "You said we would. I didn't necessarily agree."

"What's this really about? Your visit to my office last week?"

"You're not the only man in the world. If you've found someone else, good luck to you. I can find someone else, too." The voice moved closer and then suddenly, Scarlett marched around the corner, her face tight and hard. "Muriel," she said in precise voice. "You're welcome to him."

Hagen, a bare two steps behind, stopped, his face set. He stared after Scarlett and then back at Marigold. After visibly collecting himself, he eked out a smile. "There you are. I was looking for you."

Marigold stood, welded to the spot. '*If you have found someone else...*' She hoped she was smiling, though she couldn't be sure. "If you want to find women at large functions, most of us are lined up outside the loo." Her voice sounded steady, though the pulse in her neck thrummed with the beat of her heart. "The men's loos don't get the same amount of traffic. I've always thought a good designer of venues used for large functions should take a more considered approach to that sort of thing."

He hadn't explained what had happened between him and Scarlett in the office last week. Scarlett had looked smug and he had been flustered.

At the time, Marigold hadn't been overly concerned. Her employer didn't need to answer to her. Now in a relationship with him, she recognized the expression on the face of the other woman was one of humiliation. She had been supplanted. Apparently, as Sandra had originally hinted, the two had enjoyed a relationship. Marigold hadn't suspected that. Hagen had let her think he had been, until her, a bereaved widower. Apparently, she was as blind as her mother. Hardening inside, she stood straighter, chin higher.

"You're a very astute woman." He sounded a little more relaxed, though he kept his eyes on Scarlett's retreating back.

Marigold fixed her smile. "Scarlett is everywhere these days. How did she get a date with a married man from interstate?"

"I suppose she knows someone who knows someone. Isn't that the way this sort of thing usually happens?"

"Not in my world. I've never had anyone ask me to go out with a stranger. She wouldn't be working for an escort service, would she?"

He laughed, as if his dates witnessed scenes between him and his ex-lovers all the time. "I doubt it. Her divorce settlement was very generous. I think she is the sort of woman who wants to attend every function possible, and she asks around until she finds out how to wrangle an invitation."

"Do people really live like that?"

"They do in her circles. Not in mine."

Not his? Which were his circles and which were Scarlett's? In the foyer, Scarlett had said something about husbands playing around with wives' best friends. Had she been referring to herself? Sandra had said Scarlett was Mercia's friend. This would explain Hagen's caginess. Marigold should have suspected that he had been playing around outside of his marriage when she recalled his comment about having himself tested for a sexually transmitted disease.

For a man to have an STD check, he must have had some reason. He said he had been tested recently. Before or after Scarlett?

Marigold's head ached. According to Scarlett, Marigold was welcome to Hagen.

She tucked a wandering lock of her hair behind her ear, desperate to put aside thoughts about his former or current relationship with Scarlett. Having tonight ruined by the other woman was unbearable. Unable to look him in the eye, she said, "I shouldn't have chased you down, but I wanted a review of my performance tonight."

"Gold. Twenty-four carat." He fingered the top button on his jacket, as if needing something to do with his hand. "Thomas and Bertrand enjoyed themselves. You don't have the opportunity to sit beside a beautiful and intelligent woman at every corporate dinner."

"That's good to know," she said drily.

"As you can see by my partners tonight, I rarely have a chance myself." He sounded wry.

"That's even better to know." She silently added, *for the time being.* While she had Hagen, she would enjoy him without worrying about where he had been before and with whom. For tonight, at least, he was hers.

After they sat down again for a chocolate dessert that Marigold found she couldn't swallow, Kell gave an amusing talk about being the company's project manager, which raised a cheer. Calli had done well for her family in marrying him. Hagen had done well for his family in marrying Mercia.

Tiggy wouldn't let team Allbrook down, either. Marigold had no one who would be proud or ashamed of her. Her behavior would only ever reflect on her upbringing.

If the Allbrooks knew she was currently cohabiting with Hagen they would never see her the same way. Awkward wouldn't even begin to explain how that would color her relationship with them, which was why she had never even hinted to Hagen's sisters that she had a crush on him. As long as they never knew she had let them down by succumbing to her desperate feelings for him, she would be safe from losing their respect.

With this in mind, she didn't cling to him on the way out the door that night. Though he would fade out of her life too soon, she had him for tonight. Even the world's greatest cad wouldn't invite one woman to dress in his house, and wear a gown he bought, and leave a function with another.

His car slid into his garage and stopped after one last powerful sigh. He walked around and handed her out. With a careful expression on his face, he took her into his arms, and rested his face on her hair. "Watching you from the other side of the table was torture."

"Did you think I would say something tactless to embarrass you?" she asked in a dead voice.

"What brought that on? You're the one person I trust never to embarrass me. Good as gold, Marigold. Your behavior is as perfect as the way you looked tonight. If only I could sing, I would sing that to you," he added softly.

"It would echo quite bit in the garage."

He laughed and then his face turned serious. "I don't know what you heard between Scarlett and me, but sometimes she gossips too much. I would prefer her to keep private matters private."

"Nobody wants to hear gossip, unless it's about someone else. Take it that I heard nothing worthwhile." She smoothed his pale gold hair back from his face and rose to her toes to press a soft kiss on his mouth. "I felt like a princess tonight. I wouldn't have missed the function for the world. Property developing is much more interesting than I would have previously thought."

"The scale of what you previously thought being nil?"

She shook her head. "Two or three. I've given it a ranking of eight now. That's out of ten, in case you were wondering."

"What would I have to do for you to give a ranking of ten to my family's company?"

"Promote me to social director." She turned and led the way into the house. He followed her. "We don't have one. But I'll see if I can find a place."

"When I go back to my old job, I'm going to feel hard done by—no dinners, no company perks at all." She continued through the kitchen to the upstairs, her every step forced, her every thought blotted out.

Hagen kept close behind her, saying nothing. She entered the bedroom, about to head into her dressing room, but he stopped her by the bed, loosening the knot of his tie. Then he took her little bag from her and tossed it to the side of the room. "And after all the time you took to slip into the gown, I am going to take it off you inch-by-inch." His voice sounded low and husky.

Her gaze met his, and she saw on his face an expression of tenderness that she hadn't seen before. Her breath eased out in a slow sigh of helpless yearning. "I could do with a little help." Her voice trembled, and she so much wanted to be the sophisticate he would prefer—but she could be no one other than herself, a woman who had only ever loved one man, this man.

He stepped closer and held her against his big warm body while he eased down the zip of her gown. "I like your style. I always have."

"It's your style." She nuzzled her face into his neck. His golden skin tasted like salty shaving cream, which she suddenly decided she craved. "You bought this gown for me."

"Anyone could have bought the gown." His lips touched her forehead, his voice so low that he barely whispered. "Not everyone can have the woman underneath, and I don't know how I got so lucky."

"I don't know how I did, either." She lifted to her toes, her arms around his neck, while his mouth began a slow exploration of hers. At the same time, he slid her gown off her shoulders.

The weight sent the fabric to the floor in thick folds. She eased her body away from his, stepping out of the gown, keeping the gentle pressure of his lips against hers. At the same time, she began to unbutton his shirt. He had no problem whatsoever unhooking her bra, and he tossed aside the lacy scrap. For a moment, he stopped kissing her and leaned back to help her to wrestle his shirt buttons undone. Then he dragged her into the circle of his arms again, his palms settling onto the sides of her breasts.

Her nipples, squashed against the skin of his chest, began to swell and ache. He lifted her hair and kissed her neck, her shoulders, beneath her chin, and down to the tops of her breasts. At the same time, he dragged a thumb across each nipple. Sensitized, she made a sound of yearning. She stood, her hands on his broad shoulders, barely breathing, her gaze on his perfect face. His expression said he loved her, and for a moment she believed that they belonged together. She couldn't speak if she tried. Instead, she kicked off her shoes.

She wore cheap thin pantyhose, and she didn't mind a bit when he slid the fabric down with her undies. Lifting each foot out, she stood naked in his arms, warmed by his athletic body close against her. Clearly, he would remove his own trousers, but first he edged out of his shoes. He toed off his socks. She had never seen anyone do that before, and she smiled, but just once in her life she wanted to undo a man's zipper. She pushed his ready hands out of the way and did so.

"Done," she said in a strange whispery voice she hardly recognized. "My dream come true."

"Which part of this was your dream? Getting me naked? You've done that before a couple of times. It's not so hard."

"At the risk of falling into a linguistic trap, it's hard enough."

He gave a long slow smile. "Hard enough for a condom."

"Do you have one in your pocket?"

"In my back pocket." His eyebrows lifted with a clear challenge. "If you put it on me, that will be my dream come true."

She scrabbled behind him and found a line of condoms. After tearing one off, she carefully took out the fragile protection while he stepped out of his trousers and his knit boxers.

His smooth, hard penis stood erect and he breathed carefully as she rolled on the condom. Then he moved right up against her, hitching her leg over his hip, his erection hard and thick and eager. Without noticeable effort, he lifted her by the waist and landed her onto the middle of the bed, his body right on top of her with her leg still curled over his thighs.

Then he began kissing her, from her mouth to her neck, to her breasts and back again to her mouth. She squirmed with pleasure, guiding his penis into her slick folds. Instantly, her need grew desperate, and she clutched at his muscular, tight buttocks, urging him on with the pressure of her fingers. He took her lips again and slowly edged inside her, not as easily as she might have expected. Nevertheless, she arched with an almost painful pleasure, noting that her body seemed only too willing to moisten and accommodate him. Raising her pelvis, she wound her legs around his hips and took him deeper. Her fingers clenched in his hair while her body took control of her emotions, lifting and moving in counterpoint to his rhythm.

Her skin prickled with damp heat. As he began to thrust harder and faster, almost shifting her up the bed with the force, she lost control of her breathing. Gasping, she tightened around him, experiencing a peak she would rather hold back. Although she did her best to prolong the moment, her body acted independently, and she began to climax. A sound like a wail came from the back of her throat.

Hagen was still hard when she flopped, her body sated. He rose on one elbow and examined her face. "I think you could probably do that again," he said in a smoky tone.

"I couldn't. My heart would stop beating. But if you have to..." She muffled her laugh into the skin of his shoulder.

He moved her hair back off her face and gazed into her eyes. "I don't have to," he said in an uncharacteristically gruff tone. "Not if you've had enough, but I think I can make you want me again."

He slid down the bed and took her with his mouth. Her body didn't consider resisting and she climaxed again. The next time she climaxed, he came with her, inside her. Although she fell asleep almost instantly, she awoke in the middle of the night, still in his arms, a disturbing dream running through the tunnels of her mind.

In the dream, she knew where she lived but couldn't remember how to get there. She followed twisted stairs, entered various strange doorways, but whichever way she tried, she ended up in an elevator that wouldn't work without a code she didn't have. The other passengers smiled but couldn't help. Every analysis of the dream made less sense than the last. Her eyes opened to in a room full of light. And still she tried to make sense of her dream. That she needed to go home was the clearest message but why she couldn't was a mystery. Soon she would lose all these sleep memories but she stayed awake, lying on her side, watching Hagen sleeping.

He breathed deeply and regularly. She noted the thickness of his light eyelashes, the strength of his facial bones, and how his hair stayed perfectly in place. Not only was he handsome, but he was beautiful. One day he would make beautiful babies with some lucky woman who would be as golden and as gorgeous as he. He had lost that chance with Mercia's death, but his chance would come again.

Her chance with him had never been a reality. She wanted to stay with him for the rest of her life, but when she had rolled on his condom, the act had reminded her once again about the life he had led before she had begun to work for him. He had worked and played like any other man, and he'd had a wife he mourned. But he'd recently been tested for STDs. What did 'recently' mean?

At the time he told her, she had accepted his words as throwaways, proof that he was willing to make sure he wouldn't pass on any accidentally acquired disease. But he would only have had himself tested if he thought he had been at risk. In what sort of world would a happily married man be at risk? Extramarital activity would require a condom, but a married woman would more than likely be taking the contraceptive pill, and he wouldn't see the need. Would he?

Of course, this could always have been Scarlett's husband and she had been the wife who had found out, but in that case why would Hagen want her to keep the matter quiet? In conversation before the dinner, Scarlett had referred to husbands sleeping with friends of wives. Not widowers or divorcees, but husbands and wives.

Marigold had to face facts. Everything she had heard from Hagen or Scarlett pointed to them having an affair while married to other partners. Unable to shut off her thoughts, she stared at the dark ceiling. Her own father had also been a cheater. Julian had been playing around with Jane while he was married to Marigold's mother.

Marigold had always loved Hagen, but she realized she was now *in love* with him, too, which was a different matter entirely. In love meant consumed with love, achingly in love, besotted, and needy. However, she couldn't give so much of herself to a man like her father, who took commitment lightly, who saw his marriage vows as unimportant. Hoping not to wake him, she reached over to switch off the bedside lamp.

The first time she had broken up with Hagen had been bad enough. She couldn't go through those empty hours again, the crying jags, the sense of loss, almost of mourning. The second time would be worse because she now knew the depth of her love for him.

To go back to her lonely bed in her lonely house would be the hardest thing she'd ever had to do. Her mother had not fought Julian leaving her. She had let him go after barely uttering a word. Marigold wasn't her mother. She wouldn't let a man make a fool of her for years and then watch him leave anyway. Marigold would do the leaving before she had too much to lose.

Shifting away from him, she turned her back, determined not to weaken. He would survive without her, and she would survive without him. She had previously. As soon as Tiggy arrived home, Marigold would go back to her old job in property staging for someone else. She didn't have Tiggy's talent for property design.

She opened her eyes to the early morning light streaming in through the window. The bathroom door clicked open and Hagen walked out, so handsome, so tall, and so unreachable. Her heart cracked.

He gave her a long, slow, lazy smile. Dressed in a towel, his immediate thought on seeing her awake was obvious. "It's seven. We slept in."

"I can get dressed in an instant." Closing off her expression, she sat up immediately and swung her feet over the side of the bed so fast that she almost overbalanced.

He looked resigned. "I'll make breakfast while you're in the shower."

"Good idea." She found fresh underwear and her work clothes in the dressing room and transported them to the bathroom, showered, and dressed. Then she took a few minutes to pack her bag. She carried it down the stairs to the kitchen, wondering if it was ethical to let him give her breakfast when she was leaving him.

He eyed her bag. "Is bacon and eggs overkill after last night?"

"It's always overkill, but not something I have often enough to complain about." She put her bag by the garage doorway. "I'll set the table."

He turned his back and cracked the eggs into the pan. His system was messy with another pan used to fry the bacon but who was she to complain when she didn't have to clean up? While he started the bread toasting, she set the breakfast room table. The silence seemed overloaded, but perhaps because she didn't know what to say to him. On a normal morning, she would talk about the projected day. "I think we'll make it to work on time." She glanced at him.

"It doesn't matter for me, because I set my own working hours, but if you're late you'll be docked."

Her mouth twisted into a smile. "Even if I'm sleeping with the boss?"

He looked inscrutable. "If you tell everyone you're sleeping with me, that would be a different matter. Will you?"

"Of course not."

"Sit, and I'll bring over the plates." He placed her breakfast in front of her and her throat felt as if she had swallowed a tennis ball.

Her appetite deserted her. Willing herself, she loaded her fork and then she ate as fast as she could. Prolonging her time with him was too hard. "Do you want orange juice?"

"Thank you."

She scraped out her chair and left for the kitchen where she poured two glasses. He followed with the two used plates. They each drank a glass of juice while leaning against the countertop, facing but not speaking.

"What?" he finally said.

She placed her glass in the sink. "I'm leaving." She kept her back turned.

"So I imagined when I saw your bag. Why?"

She shrugged. "I don't like the idea of sleeping with the boss's son for a promotion."

"Is that what you were doing?"

She slowly turned and met his gaze. "Not initially, no, but last night you said you would find a better job for me. Would you have said that if I wasn't about to leap into bed with you?"

He stared into her eyes, his expression a mask. "I wasn't serious."

She hardened her heart. "You were using your position for your own purposes."

His voice deepened. "Tell me the truth."

"Maybe I was simply reliving the past, seeing if I made a mistake the first time around," she said, wearily. "But I didn't. We don't share the same values. Aside from that, this was a fling. You're a good-looking man, and I was lonely."

"You're a good-looking woman, and I was lonely, too. I thought we had something going for us."

"I'm really not your type. I'm not sophisticated enough."

His mouth formed a grim line and his eyes turned a hard shade of blue. "I'll see you at work then." Losing her gaze, he moved across her to rinse his glass.

"I hope this won't—"

"No, it won't. We need you until Tiggy gets back."

She swallowed and grabbed up her bag on the way to her car in the garage, glad he hadn't extended the moment. Now she only had to face him at work but she suspected he could evade her easily enough. They'd already had to try to find moments together at AA & Co.

She arrived before he did, of course. He would give her a head start so that she could be out of his way when he set foot into his office.

"Morning," Sandra said, lifting her head and smiling. "How was last night?"

"The dinner? Elegant. Enlightening." Marigold's voice came out husky.

A crease formed between Sandra's eyebrows. "How is Hagen this morning?"

"You'll have to ask him."

"Oh. Right." Sandra went back to her typing.

Sitting at her desk, Marigold tried to concentrate on her next design for the school gymnasium. AA wanted four single-bedroom units, but she had the idea that the other occupants of the development wouldn't like student accommodation so close by. She had meant to discuss this with Hagen. Now she couldn't. She also couldn't concentrate. She kept imagining him with Scarlett. The other woman was sophisticated, beautifully dressed, and would match his lifestyle the way Mercia had.

Marigold's eyes hurt. She heard his voice in the vestibule. His door clicked shut. Safe to leave, she moved swiftly past Sandra, who said, "Hagen said he enjoyed last night, too. Then he slammed into his office. Maybe the drinks were spiked."

Marigold frowned at Sandra. "The drinks were elegant."

"So, the guests were enlightening?"

"Some were, yes." Marigold stalked off to the staff room. Coffee would help her concentration. She switched on the machine and waited.

Demi walked into the room, carrying a cardboard tray of sweet things. "Morning, darling. Did you have a good time last night?"

"Sure did," Marigold said with faked enthusiasm. "You must have sprung out of bed before daylight to have made all those."

"The pastries? I buy them from a nice little Greek bakery."

"Why did I have the idea that you did all this yourself?"

"I used to, but Mercia, my darling ex-daughter-in-law said it was mumsy when I could buy pastries every bit as good and save myself the time."

"Mumsy? And you accepted that?" Marigold frowned. She couldn't imagine perfect Mercia saying anything quite so crass.

"In a way, she made sense." Demi sighed. "I still make everything for my family, but it was time consuming to keep the office supplied as well. Not all her ideas were bad, though. To change a subject I shouldn't be discussing, you and Hagen looked perfect together last night, Marigold. Your bright hair and his light hair, well, you make the perfect golden couple. Hagen had a hard time trying not to look besotted."

Marigold cleared her throat. "I'm sure he didn't. Looks are deceiving. I think you might have the wrong idea about us. We have a working relationship. It would be poor form to mix work with pleasure."

"I know, darling, but sometimes these things can't be helped. He has watched you with hungry eyes since he was eighteen. That's more than ten years."

"He hasn't seen me for six of them." Marigold crossed her arms.

"That's his pride."

"He married Mercia."

Demi sighed. "There's no denying he made a mistake or two. But I mustn't interfere. He has made a mess of his life, and I thought…"

"He made a mess of his life?" Marigold blinked in amazement.

Demi lifted her shoulders. "I will say no more on the subject. Not that I actually know a lot more. Hagen has been a mystery to me since he was born. He's the strong and silent type like his father. Though, I always did like a good mystery," she ended in a vague voice. "Oh, I've forgotten the pods for the coffee machine. I must go out to the car to get them."

Rubbing her forehead, Marigold watched her leave. Hagen's mother thought he had made a mess of his life? Perfect, golden boy Hagen? As far as Marigold could see, Hagen had had his golden life blessed since the minute of his birth—except for the loss of Mercia.

She wandered back to Tiggy's office, her coffee in her hand, deciding to forget Sandra asking her how Hagen was this morning. His assistant had made a silly slip of the tongue. She couldn't possibly suspect that good-as-gold Marigold was sleeping with her boss.

Chapter 12

Hagen's mother burst into his office. He'd immersed himself in paperwork since he had arrived this morning. Every time he came up for air, he thought about Marigold. Not for a moment did he believe she had moved out because he had considered finding her a more suitable job with the company. If she had honestly wanted one, she could be slotted in, but she had decided to wipe him out of her life for another reason entirely. She wouldn't risk loving anyone. And, unfortunately, he understood.

Ma planted herself onto his black bench seat and crossed her legs as if she meant to stay for a while. "We need to talk." Her mouth firmed.

He didn't want to talk. He wanted to act, but he couldn't grab Marigold and tell her he loved her and that he had never loved anyone but her. She didn't trust him now any more than she had the first time she had tossed him aside. Although he hadn't known about her mother's deteriorating condition, Marigold had assumed he wouldn't have supported her during her mother's long illness. She could have been right, but he wanted to think she was wrong. However, after living in a household where the women outnumbered the men, he knew telling one she was wrong would get him exactly nowhere.

This time he knew she was wrong. And she was lying. She had reverted to Marigold-mode and used words to distance herself from him, assuming that like her father, at the click of another's woman's fingers, Hagen would pack up and leave. He loved her, but so far he had done a hopeless job of showing her that. He needed to tell her instead. Right now. With only Marigold on his mind, he rose to his feet to usher his mother out of the room.

Ma held up a stopping palm. "Sit, please. I have something to say, and I'm not leaving until I've said it. This morning, I accidentally told Marigold that you used to be besotted with her. She seemed surprised."

He shrugged. "And?"

"Oh, you're as bad as she is." She firmed her lips. "I don't know why Tiggy bothered giving up her job for Marigold if you didn't intend to do something about her."

He frowned. "About Tiggy or Marigold?"

"What could you do about Tiggy? Don't answer. I mean about Marigold. We thought if we got you two into a situation where you had to speak, you would resolve whatever needed to be resolved. Last night, it looked as though you had."

"I thought we had." He sat on his desk chair, rubbing his forehead and staring into his mother's earnest brown eyes. "But we were a social situation. Marigold is always beautifully behaved in company." He tried to outstare his mother, also a waste of his time.

Ma offered him a reproving smile. "She is, isn't she? It's a shame she doesn't handle her private life as well."

"I doubt that you interfering will help."

She let out a weighted sigh. "We got you two talking again, didn't we? Therefore, I'll give you my unsolicited advice. If you want Marigold, now is the time, Hagen. You won't keep getting opportunities with her. She is a highly intelligent woman. She won't wait forever for you."

"Hah."

"And what is that supposed to mean?"

"She has already decided I'm not for her."

"Of course you are."

He stared at the papers on his desk. "You tell her. She won't believe me."

Ma pulled her chin back. "Well, she won't if you tell her. You have to show her."

"I did show her. I didn't tell her, but I'm not giving up this time, or not without a good try."

"I'm glad to hear that. She is not at all confident. Mercia has given her a lot to compete with."

"I thought you didn't like Mercia."

"She was beautiful, confident, and, well, beautiful." Ma lifted her shoulders.

"I love seeing you trying to be tactful." He almost smiled. "Mercia was loud, opinionated, and rude to you. Do you think I didn't know? I assumed she would be right for me, as my opposite. You always said I was too reserved."

"And she made you more reserved. She alienated your family, and we thought for a while we would lose you. I know you don't like hearing this. I know you were always loyal to her and although I wish you hadn't been, I do admire you for that. But you have a chance to start again, and I don't want you closing in on yourself and not taking the opportunity we presented to you."

"We?" He rubbed the back of his neck. "Tiggy presented this opportunity by taking an unwanted holiday?"

"If we couldn't get Marigold out of her house, we could never put you two back together again. Tiggy hoped Marigold wouldn't be able to refuse her if she asked for a favor."

"And she didn't."

"It was a good idea of Tiggy's," Ma said defensively. "We hadn't been able to get you two together previously. Before you married Mercia, we asked you to dinner and we asked Marigold to dinner but as soon as either of you heard the other had been asked, you backed out for some flaky reason or another. That's when I started getting suspicious. Something must have happened between you."

"Nothing much happened between us. We were just beginning when her mother got sick. She couldn't deal with both of us at the same time."

Ma inclined her head to the side. "That's understandable. Taking on a serious relationship would have been difficult at that stage."

"Especially taking on me and my oversized ego."

"Now, now. You were no worse than any other rich man's son."

With a wry smile, he lifted his shoulders. "We do our best but we weren't the ones who made the millions. We either have to spend it, lose it, or prove we deserve our privileged positions. We have our families' reputations to carry and at that stage I wasn't sure I was good enough."

"Possibly she picked up on that, but you're older now and your father and I are very proud of the man you have become. He won't have any misgivings about leaving the company in your capable hands."

For a moment he dropped his gaze, stunned by the praise. He knew he worked hard, but taking over the family company had always seemed a distant aim. He had grown emotionally since Mercia had died. Now he was ready to take what he wanted from life. And what he wanted was Marigold by his side, supporting him as she had at his dinner party, and as she had last night. He nodded and stood. "Conversation over. Thanks for your input. You have helped me straighten out my mind."

"So you will tell Marigold you love her?"

"That's what I meant to do before you plonked yourself into that chair."

"Tell her she made last night a delightful social occasion for the lucky investors who sat either side of her. I saw each of them laughing. No one ever laughed when they sat with Mercia," Ma said, and she left with her head held high.

No one had laughed with Mercia because she'd always found business dinners a chore. Marigold didn't. She liked people, and she shone during social events, which was why he had insisted on waltzing with her at his last school formal. He shouldn't have, but just once he had wanted everyone to notice how special she was. Soon enough someone more worthy than he would carry her off. Hagen would be too busy trying to live up to his family's expectations to find time to woo anyone.

And now he had to work out a way to win her, his golden delight.

He prepared himself with two deep breaths, rose and left the office, meaning to stroll into Marigold's. Sandra arose from her desk as he shut his door behind him. "I hope she gave you a good talking to."

"Who? My mother?"

She lowered her head and looked at him over her glasses. "Someone needed to wake you up to yourself."

"I had every intention of waking myself up," he said in a mild voice.

"I hope you're not going to make matters worse."

He examined the wary expression on her face. "How loud was our conversation?"

"I've been sitting outside your door for four years." Her eyebrows wriggled. "You don't always close it properly and neither did your wife when she visited, and she had a propensity to be loud. In that time, I've heard a lot. I hope you are planning on telling Marigold the truth. You won't win her with evasions, like you can with your mother."

"I didn't evade anything," he answered defensively.

"Oh, yes you did. You always stick up for Mercia. That's not a bad thing in itself, but I've heard much too much to believe what you want everyone to believe. In a way, I was sorry for her but that doesn't excuse her behavior."

He firmed his jaw. "I'm not about to discuss Mercia with Marigold."

"I think you have to. She has the wrong idea entirely."

He scratched his eyebrow. "Without any of you knowing my business, you are all determined to tell me how to run it," he said, exasperated.

"Because you're doing such a bad job on your own."

"So, tell Marigold the truth? She has never asked me for the truth."

"You haven't let her close enough. She is a woman who needs closeness. Tell her everything, Hagen. You might even discuss your feelings, though that's a hard ask."

"Could you do one thing for me?" he asked politely. "Take yourself off for half an hour."

She turned back to her desk, opened the bottom drawer, removed her handbag, and said, "If you make a mess of this, I'll resign."

"You're fortunate that I want to keep you." He watched her march off and then he took a breath deep enough to feel in his toes and knocked on Marigold's door.

"Come in. Oh, Hagen." Her mouth curled into a wary smile. "This is going to be awkward, I suspect."

"Not at all." He drew the visitor's chair up to her desk and sat. "I've been given two sets of unsolicited advice this morning. My mother thinks I should explain my feelings toward you, and Sandra thinks I'm going to stuff this up."

She drew her eyebrows together. "What have you been saying about us?"

"I was wondering what you'd been telling them."

"Not a word."

"Then apparently, our relationship isn't as secret as we presumed. Sandra insists that I tell you the truth. Which do you want to hear first, truth or feelings?"

"Neither. I'm okay, truly. I can keep running on the spot here trying to do what Tiggy does so easily. Or, if it's too awkward keeping me here, I can leave. Maybe Tiggy will come back if you ask her?"

He heaved a sigh. "Good change of subject, but I'll start by telling you about my marriage." Leaning back, he folded his arms across his chest before he realized that defending himself should be the last thing on his mind. "Sandra thinks you have the wrong idea about Mercia. I have never discussed my late wife with you, therefore I don't know what idea you have." He hauled in a breath and made sure he looked Marigold right in the eye, determined to tell the unvarnished truth. "I married her because she was there. No other reason. She wanted me, she was bright, good-looking, and had a wonderful social life. I didn't. Study and work was about all I did. I had my father's expectations to reach. Even before the wedding I was having second thoughts."

"Are you sure you want to tell me this? I don't think it's any of my business."

"I'll cut to the chase. I was a very bad husband. I ignored my wife most of the time because she and her shallow friends bored me. When I realized I was wasting my life and hers, I asked her for a divorce. She said *absolutely not* and was so traumatized by the suggestion that she had to get away for the weekend. Next thing, I had a police officer at the front door telling me she'd been killed in a car crash on a country road. The man in the following car stopped to help, the officer was glad to say. That man was Scarlett's husband."

Marigold moistened her lips. "You assumed she was about to spend the weekend with him. Him being there might have been pure coincidence."

He kept his gaze on her.

Marigold breathed out. "And Scarlett knew."

"Not until he was questioned as a witness. Then he told her the affair had been ongoing for months. So, she asked for a divorce. She and I agreed to keep the matter quiet. I have been a grieving widower for a year, and now I want my life back."

She sat, her gaze on his, her jaw loose. Then she swallowed. "Oh, dear. You did a very good job of being a grieving widower."

"I couldn't be sure initially that she hadn't driven into the tree on purpose. It didn't make me feel too noble."

"Divorce or death? That doesn't sound like a sensible option. Either way she lost."

"And I keep thinking that rather than lose, she wanted it all, the rich husband and the lover on the side." Leaning forward, he rested his forearms on her desk, keeping his gaze on hers. "He, Scarlett's husband, said a kangaroo hit the car, and Mercia skidded into a tree. Investigations proved that, but it took a while."

"If anyone other than Scarlett knows Mercia was having an affair with her husband, they certainly haven't gossiped about it."

"I wouldn't be surprised if she let it slip to a few people, though no one has mentioned it to me. Sandra knows because she occasionally has to read my e-mails, but I trust her."

"Why did you insist on keeping this quiet?"

"Pride. The whole thing is tawdry." He reached across the top of the desk and took her hands in his. "I didn't ever consider showing righteous indignation. If I had been a better husband, she wouldn't have gone scouting around for other men. And there were others."

She audibly dragged in a breath. Her eyes widened and then she blinked the gloss away. "Ah. That explains the STD test," she said, dropping her gaze. "I'm sorry, Hagen. I misjudged you."

"And you ought to be sorry. If I hadn't decided not to let you misjudge me again, we might now be going our own merry ways again, too."

"I thought telling me the truth was Sandra's idea."

"Well, if Sandra hadn't decided to interfere we might not have a chance at a do-over. So, that's her brief out of the way. Next is my mother's—how

I feel about you. Starting from the bottom, I love your toes and your feet and your legs."

She blinked. Her mouth relaxed. "I kind of like yours, too," she said in a soft voice.

He smoothed his thumbs across the back of her hands. "And I love your eyes and your nose and your mouth."

"Although I hate to admit it, I like your hair quite a lot."

"What about my legs and feet?"

"I don't think that's romantic." A tiny smile formed on her face, and she gripped his fingers.

"I think it's more romantic than talking about my masculine attributes."

"I don't talk about them."

He bent and lifted her hands to his mouth. He kissed the back of each. "But most of all, apart from the rest of your body, I love you, good-as-gold Marigold."

"And that is the reason why we can't continue having an affair. Because I'm as good as gold." She sighed. "I thought trying to be the sort of woman a man would have an affair with would be titillating but it's not."

"Thank you."

"Oh, that part was good." Her mouth pursed. "It was the secret aspect that didn't suit me. I want to be with a man who doesn't need to hide. I'm not naturally sneaky."

"You're right, and I'm glad we ended the affair. We're not good at it. I thought no one knew but, apparently, everyone does. You're going to have to make an honest man of me."

She gave a wry smile. "Make you confess to everyone? I'd much rather you didn't. We'll still be meeting from time to time, and I really don't want people looking at me trying to see my reaction."

"You've forced my hand. You'll have to marry me."

She pulled back, her eyes wide and her jaw loose. "I will not."

"Don't say that. I love every scrap of you and if you don't marry me, I'll spend forever wondering what I should have done or said to convince you otherwise."

Her shoulders lost rigidity. "You want to marry me?"

"That's what happens when you fall in love. And I fell in love years ago. Marrying you was my plan from the start, but we had a few hurdles to cross."

"Jump. Hurdles to jump."

"Marry me, Marigold. Please. Then you can correct my grammar." He stood, walked around the edge of the desk, urged her to her feet, and took her into his arms.

She rested her palm flat on his cheek, while she stared directly into his eyes. "Are you sure you're not just trying to get a better deal on the redecoration of your house?"

"If I hadn't been trying to get you into my bedroom, I could have had Tiggy do it. I wanted it done your way because I planned to have you living there."

"You should have said so." Her mouth softened.

"I didn't want to frighten you off. I thought when the house was perfect, you would be sure to say yes."

"You did not." She looked as if she might finally laugh.

"I was certainly thinking along those lines. Be gentle with me. I'm only a man."

"Knock, knock, is this door open?"

"No, Ma. Not yet. She still hasn't said she will marry me."

"Do you need help in there?"

"I'm not sure you standing outside the door and listening is helping."

"I'll go away then."

"Demi!" Marigold pulled her hands out of his grip. "Don't leave. I sort of said yes."

The door opened. Demi walked in, followed by Sandra. Both were beaming.

"Are you going to plan the wedding?" Sandra asked Demi.

"I hope so. Darling Marigold doesn't have a mother, and I think I should. Don't you, Hagen?"

He glanced at Marigold. "Okay with you?"

Her expression combining a touch of puzzlement with a wryly pleased smile, she said, "No wonder you guys are so successful in business. Yes. And yes, Hagen." Her face softened. "I will marry you."

And then he had to wait for Sandra and his mother to hug each other, hug Marigold, and hug him before they left, before he got to kiss Marigold properly.

* * * *

The day before the wedding, during the final staging of her house for sale, Marigold said to Tiggy, who was helping, "I'm wondering. Would you have come back if I had made a mess of the school duplex?"

"Of course not, because you wouldn't make a mess. You're a perfectionist, Marigold. You would make sure you got it right. Aside from that, Kell was watching your back. If you'd started to flounder, Calli would have dropped by to give you a few hints. Of course, we all hoped that Hagen would."

"He has done staging, too?" Marigold widened her eyes in astonishment.

"No, but he has seen enough of it to know what to do."

"I'm beginning to think that he didn't need me to redo his house." Marigold used an indignant voice.

"He certainly did. I don't know that he much cares about the place for himself. His house was too cold the way it was. He needed his house to suit you. You're a warmer person."

Marigold had already noted that Hagen's family made sure of never criticizing Mercia. None knew she had been an unfaithful wife and would probably never find out.

Marigold liked that about Hagen. He didn't need to put others down to bring himself up. He was noble, honest, generous, and the most loving man she had ever met. No one could be less like her father. Coming from a big happy family, Hagen had no objection to expanding it. Her own dysfunctional family had been invited to her wedding. Hagen even tolerated her father and seemed to think she ought to try for a relationship with her brothers. Maybe she would.

At last she had pleased her father. Apparently marrying a handsome and wealthy man hadn't been expected of her.

"Good thing I gave you that dinner set," he said to her in all seriousness. She didn't contradict him. A little less rigidity on her part wouldn't go astray. Now that she was deliriously happy herself, she was content to let everyone else around her be happy, too.

"I hope I'm in on the plot to get you married off, too." She grinned at Tiggy. "That should be as much fun for me as your family's plotting to get Hagen married off to me."

"There had better not be a plot," Tiggy said in a dark tone, planting her fists on her hips. "I don't think I'm cut out for marriage. I'm having too much fun as a single."

Marigold could never have said that about herself. "I thought being single had been hard work, but at least I ended up with the man I love."

Tiggy hugged her. "And we get to keep you."

Marigold still hadn't found out where Tiggy had been for that six weeks she had disappeared. Tiggy had arrived within a week of Marigold's wedding announcement, and taken back her job. Now Marigold's only function was to coordinate events, which she much preferred. With Demi's help, she was organizing her wedding, which the Allbrook's insisted would be big and white, paid for by them, and used as a publicity opportunity for Allbrook's.

"Neither of the twins would consent to this, Marigold, and we're very grateful you are being so gracious," Demi had said, blinking with emotion.

Gracious? Marigold was well aware that she was marrying gold. Reminded, she said, "I'll need to put the Doulton dinner set in my car before I forget."

"Have you two finished?" Hagen strolled through the open front door.

"Pretty well." She turned and grinned at him.

"This is my last opportunity to kiss you before tomorrow." Hagen swooped Marigold into his arms, settled her there, stared into her eyes, sighed, and gave her the sort of kiss that wouldn't embarrass an onlooker, although it lasted a beat too long.

She leaned back, smiling at the only man she had ever loved. "After that, I'm yours forevermore."

"You and your dining chairs," he said, his autocratic eyebrows elevated. Behind him Billy and Joe darkened the doorway. "I couldn't think how else to get them other than to marry you."

"Come on, you two, we've got work to do." Billy pushed into the house, Joe following.

Standing in the delightful circle of Hagen's arms, she watched her chairs leaving for his house—soon hers. Tonight, she would stay with the Allbrooks, and tomorrow she would leave for her honeymoon in Paris. "We're getting Tiggy married off next," she said comfortably.

"Welcome to the family." He laughed and spun her in the direction of the front door. "When will we discuss how many children we are having?"

"Out of the way," Billy said. "Or we'll never get this done."

"I, too, thought we'd never get this done," Hagen whispered into Marigold's hair. "But now you're my very own. Good-as-gold Marigold."

Sets Appeal

A Romance By Design romance by Virginia Taylor!

In the cosmopolitan coastal city of Adelaide in South Australia, two theater lovers create a little drama of their own . . .

Twenty-seven-year-old divorcée Vix Tremain finally has her first job—as a theater-set painter—and is ready to leave the past behind. What better way to get her confidence back than a fling with a handsome stranger? She isn't looking for anything emotional, she's had enough heartbreak. Rugged Jay Dee, the set construction manager, fits the bill for no strings fun perfectly. What Vix doesn't realize is that Jay is not exactly a stranger . . .

Jay would recognize wealthy, spoiled Vix anywhere. After all, she's the ex-wife of the man who destroyed his career. Naturally, Jay wants a little sweet revenge—at first. To his surprise, Vix is far from the ice princess he expected, and spending time with her changes everything. Soon he realizes he's actually falling for the vulnerable beauty. But becoming entangled with her will mean revealing who he is—and opening them both up to more pain. With their dreams at stake, is their connection strong enough to weather the truth—and take center stage?

Chapter 1

Her shoulders almost creaking with tension, Victoria Tremain turned off her car engine. Tonight, as one of the crew, she had attended the first party she had been to in a year, a pre-production getting-to-know-you function held for the cast and crew of the stage version of *High Society*. Experiencing a deadly case of stage fright, she aimed the huge smile she had plastered on her face in the direction of her wildly attractive passenger. He had told her he would make her a cup of coffee if she drove him home.

Behind him, the blaring streetlight reflected on the outside of a suburban redbrick bungalow with no fence and a front garden that had been dug over but not planted—a work in progress, but not out of place in this narrow street of tidy post-war houses. Shadowy stacks of planks lay in his concrete driveway.

"So, this is where you build your theater sets?" Her voice sounded suitably low and husky, not because she was at all sophisticated, but because she was terrified.

Picking up men wasn't as easy as... Actually, she hadn't imagined picking up men would be easy, not for someone as naturally awkward as she. She had almost fallen over her feet in her hurry to get the hunky set-builder into her car. Or maybe she almost fell over her big yellow heels, which took some getting used to—for she was now flashy, single, champagne-drinking Vix Tremain, trying to find the life she had missed during the past seven years. Married at the age of twenty, she had divorced eleven months ago.

He shook his head. "The wood belongs in the garage, but I haven't had time yet to shift it." Muffled *doof-doof* music rocked the air as he opened the car door on his side.

She opened her side, stepped out, and caught her bag on the handbrake. Muttering under her breath, she untangled the strap and closed the door, hoping he hadn't noticed. His coordination was as notable as his big, honed body.

She cleared her throat. "When did you finish your last set?" Scooping her hair back, she followed him along an overgrown path to the low front porch. "A couple of weeks ago. My team does four a year." He fumbled for his keys.

A sudden gust of wind blew a sheet of newspaper across the road and an orphaned takeaway coffee cup rattled against the fence. As she took a step back to give him space, her spiked heel caught between two slats and she stumbled.

He grabbed her, steadying her against his chest, his shaggy brown hair idly teasing across her cheek. "My woman trap." He set her back on her own feet. Suppressed laughter deepened his voice.

She gave a careful smile, scoring herself a ten for not apologizing. The man smelled like pine chips and the fresh sea breeze blowing in from the port. He opened the door, a forest green blistered over white undercoat and slivers of ashen wood. For a moment, his arm blocked her as he reached around his doorframe for the light. The pulse in her neck thudding, she waited until he stepped back. This could be her first one-night stand if she didn't mess up or say something dorky. Tonight, she had great expectations of herself. She had scrubbed-up quite well and now she only had to follow through.

He placed his hand on the center of her back and guided her through a bare hallway to an open space containing a sitting room at one end and a dining–slash–kitchen area at the other. Tossing his leather jacket over a chair, he stepped behind the kitchen countertop and began to pour coffee beans into a grinder sitting beside a basic espresso machine. For a moment, she experienced stark disappointment. Perhaps when he had said "coffee," he had meant "coffee."

"Take a seat." Using his eyes, he indicated the sitting area, painted in faded magnolia and furnished with a floral two-seater couch and a couple of stiff-backed chairs upholstered in gray.

Keeping him in view, she sat on the edge of the couch, clutching her handbag to her chest. Her mouth was as dry as the recent winter. "What's your real name?"

"JD." Resting his work-roughened hands on the countertop, he flitted his gaze over her legs.

Her skirt had hitched up too high. She thought about using her handbag as a cover but she had worn the bad-girl, tight red skirt to change her image. Breathing out, she put the bag on the floor, giving him a sideways glance. "I'm guessing. An abbreviation of Juvenile Delinquent?" She held her breath.

He smiled, forming creases that were almost dimples. "From *West Side Story*?" He scooped the ground beans into the measure.

She half-relaxed. He recognized the musical, and most men didn't. "Just Deciding might suit you better." She laughed at her blatant hint but when his gaze connected with hers, her face warmed. He could take all the time he needed and if he didn't plan on having sex with her, the world wouldn't end. He might simply have wanted a comfortable ride home. Men invariably preferred using her cars.

Fortunately, he gave her an amused look. Reaching for the mugs, he showed her an impressive back view, wide at the top and angling to lean hips and a tight, hard rear. Although stacked, he couldn't be called handsome. The left side of his face had been puckered by a scar that wove up his cheek and toward his eye. He looked like the tradesman he was, an appearance he emphasized with his faded jeans and cotton shirt.

"How do you like your coffee?" He stared at her over his shoulder.

"Plain black, please."

At the party for *High Society*, she'd used champagne to segue into the new sophisticated Vix Tremain. Awkward, tactless Victoria Nolan had barely spoken to a man in this past year, let alone stumbled into his house. Married young, she'd never ventured into the dating scene. Instead, she had accepted the first man who had shown an interest in her, impressionable fool that she had been. "How complicated was your last set?"

"A single room." He shrugged. "Three entrances and a flight of stairs." He brought over a brimming coffee, placing the mug on the blue-painted table adjacent to her seat.

"Sit here," she said, amazing herself by patting the cushion beside her. She even considered adding a casual touch by kicking off her heels, but couldn't with any semblance of grace. Her legs were long and her skirt was a size tighter than she usually bought. She should have worn fitted pants. Then she could have crossed her legs or casually hooked one up onto the couch. Dressing to pick up a man needed more planning than she had imagined. She dragged in a breath. "I see we have ten scene changes. That's enough to keep me painting solidly for the next three months."

He lowered himself beside her. For a few heartbeats, he sat silently. "Are you being paid for your time or the job?"

"For the job. My specialty is set design, but I've never worked. I have to start. So, I thought taking on the painting first would ease my way in, which makes the money immaterial."

He gave an almost imperceptible nod. "When did it happen?"

"Getting the job?"

"I'm asking about your divorce." He lifted her third finger, left hand, which still held an indented reminder of the wedding ring she no longer wore.

She no longer owned the platinum band, either. Although she should have flushed the meaningless thing into the sewer, she couldn't stand waste. Instead, she had gone out to buy herself a box of celebration chocolates, the last she had eaten since then, and sold the ring, dropping the money into the hat of the first street musician she saw on the way back to her car.

"You're observant. I've been free for a year."

"Good."

She tilted her head to the side, trying an unconcerned smile. "Because?"

His eyebrows lifted.

Her insides began to quiver with hope.

He settled his arm along the back of the couch. His hand touched her hair, and he tugged a lock. "What am I going to do with you?" He used a deep, soft tone.

"Did you have anything else in mind when you offered to make me coffee?" Her tentative gaze met his.

"Not my thinking mind, no."

"Your thinking mind as compared to…?"

He drew air through his teeth. "As compared to the mind I don't often use when I'm with a beautiful woman. So..." He rested one large hand on the side of her neck and his thumb under her jaw. Leaning over, he touched his lips to hers.

A delicious shiver ran though her. His eyelashes were thick and brown at the tips and blond near his lids.

When she could breathe evenly, she said, "You have nice, soft lips."

"That's my line." His steady gaze held hers.

"I thought you might need encouragement."

His mouth tilted at the corners and his eyes gleamed. "More likely discouragement."

She gave an off-hand shrug, smiling inside. "I'm just not in the mood to do that," she said, trying for a mock snooty tone.

"To discourage me?" He glanced sideways at her. "Let me get this straight. You want to encourage me?"

"I drove you home. What would you expect if you had driven me home?" She lifted her eyebrows.

He nodded. "I would hope for much more than a cup of coffee."

She couldn't look away from him, and she certainly couldn't breathe.

He meshed his fingers with hers. "And, fair's fair." Staring at her face, he put his other arm along the back of the couch behind her. His hand shifted to the nape of her neck and she found herself tucked into his frame.

She glanced up, hoping to be kissed again.

He obliged, dropping his mouth lightly over hers and testing her upper lip with his tongue.

She drew back. "The bedroom?"

"Right now?"

Experimentally, she brushed his upper thigh with her knuckles, noting an exciting shape expanding his jeans. "I can't possibly give you time to change your mind."

He picked up her hand and gently took the pad of her forefinger between his lips. "Why hurry? We're going to be working together," he said in a relaxed voice.

"Not often. When your job ends, mine begins. I can't paint a set before it's built."

He toyed with her fingers.

She wriggled uncomfortably. "If you're afraid of awkwardness when we meet again, I'm sure we will hardly ever meet again. I mean…"

"So, you want to get into bed with someone that you expect to hardly ever meet again?"

Her insides began to shake. "If you don't want to, you can say no. I thought… Well, it's kind of normal, isn't it, to have an instant physical attraction to someone? Well, it's not normal for me, but…"

He leaned back, staring into her eyes. "I didn't plan on saying no."

"Are we arguing about what happens next, or are we agreeing?" She started to chew on her lip and, mindful of looking insecure, stopped.

He glanced away. "What color are my eyes?"

"You have light brown hair, so you probably have light eyes."

"Your eyes are blue."

"You're looking straight at them now," she said indignantly.

"How does that follow? You're not naturally blond."

"I almost am."

He laughed.

Embarrassed, for she had been born blond and had remained that way until about the age of ten, when her hair had turned a pure shade of natural mouse, she said, "Hardly anyone is at my age. If you are only interested in natural blondes, you're doomed to disappointment."

"I didn't say I was disappointed. My mind was simply trying to connect eye color and hair color."

"I can only judge your reaction to me by your, um..." She stopped, knowing she shouldn't tell a man that from the moment they'd met, his smile had lured her on, way past her normal comfort zone. Most men preferred assured women who knew how to tease.

"My *um*?" His expression blanked, and he stood.

Her stomach dropped to her toes. Being knocked back on her first try at propositioning a man would probably put her off ever trying again. Any other unnatural blonde in a tight red skirt would get the man she wanted... or leave with her dignity intact. She rose to her feet, avoiding his eyes. "So, I'll say goodnight and thank you for the coffee."

He stood. "You read my *um* right. That's one of the disadvantages of being male."

She nodded, reaching for her handbag. A tall, confident man like him was possibly propositioned twice a day, at least. He could afford to pick and choose. Her breath stopped as she realized what he had implied and, her mouth not quite shut, she lifted her gaze to his.

"And thank me in the morning," he murmured as his mouth slowly connected with hers.

At first stunned, she didn't respond. Then he settled a palm on the small of her back, drawing her close. Her insides began to hum, and she leaned away to struggle out of her jacket. He helped, tossing the distraction onto the chair with his. She started to work on the button of his jeans, her brain a maze of unfinished thoughts. Unfortunately, in her confusion, she tangled her fingers against his flat belly.

"I'll do that," he said, his eyes glinting with humor. "I think I ought to head for the bathroom for a condom. The bedroom is through there." He indicated the room in the hallway closest to the front door.

She glanced at his chin, traced her gaze over his scar, and straightened her shoulders. Then, picking up her jacket and her bag, she went into his bedroom, where after undressing quickly, she arranged herself in his bed. With her arms at her sides, she lay staring at the flaky ceiling, forcing in long, deep breaths. He gave her time enough to ease the nervous flutter in her chest and time enough to justify acting out of character.

She had never before let anyone think they owed her a favor. A good girl all her life, she had been called prissy and conventional. She'd watched the bad girls grab whatever they wanted while she'd stood back and hoped to be valued for being honest. No more.

She'd been cheated on, taken advantage of, and left humiliated. If she had any sort of courage, she would stop living for tomorrow and start living for today—tonight. What sort of person had no regrets? Wincing, she glanced at her clothes on the floor. If need be she could make a quick getaway.

In half an hour, with luck, she would find out if sex with a wildly attractive bad boy would change her attitude. She didn't care about competing with other more attractive, more confident women, and she didn't hope for love. One single bout of satisfying sex would do her. Then, she would know she was not as frigid, repressed, and sexless as she had been told.

Staring at the door, she waited for the big, inscrutable hunk.

* * * *

Jay shut the bathroom door behind him. Last year, he had built the set for *South Pacific*. Although he hadn't attended any rehearsals of the show, while he had been bumping-in the set, he had heard an actor going over a schmaltzy song about spotting a woman across a crowded room and falling instantly in love.

Jay hadn't fallen instantly in love with Vix Tremain, but lust had featured strongly. Spotting the blonde, he had pushed through the usual crowd to introduce himself to a sleek beauty who seemed genuinely glad to talk him. Normally a woman with skin as smooth as rich cream and a long-legged, toned body would act like a show pony, but she had a rare natural charm. She also showed a clear interest in him, demonstrated by the odd self-conscious gesture, like touching her hair and moistening her lips. Every move of hers reflected his purely animal attraction. He'd thought the last theater set he ever meant to construct would easily be his most interesting.

Set painters could be anyone—male or female, old or young, ultra-serious, control freaks, or dreadlocked posers. Not often did he get assigned to a beautiful woman who looked as interested in messing around as he was. He didn't have the time for a relationship, but he could fit in a casual affair that lasted the length of the production, and he could certainly handle one with a golden man-toy. He'd been blatant about his attraction to her, and he'd intimated that a sweaty night would be had by all if she accompanied him home.

The dazzling smile she gave him in response hit him like a punch to the head. He'd seen that smile before. Only last year, when skimming the newspaper, he'd noted a photograph of the Nolans, plain, plump Victoria with her incredible smile and her older husband, Timothy, architect and millionaire entrepreneur.

Jay ran his fingers over the scar on his cheek, a memento from her husband. For at least a year, he'd thought about revenge on Timmy-boy. Although Jay was visibly scarred, he'd never been handsome. Nor did he make his living out of his looks. Bygones had been bygones, but knowing she was Tim's ex added to her appeal. In fact, he'd seen screwing her as some sort of compensation for having his future screwed by Tim. His dick had largely guided these self-serving thoughts.

Now, although still influenced by a keen body part, he found he couldn't use Vix in an act of silent revenge. Perhaps if she had been the woman he'd always assumed she was, a rich bitch with haughty opinions, he wouldn't have changed sides, but a sophisticated man-toy she was not. Instead, she was bright and wryly funny, both of which he found more sexually stimulating than a bored divorcée looking for a night on the wild side.

Crap! He couldn't knock back a woman with so little confidence in herself. If he had her, he would be all kinds of a heel. If he didn't, he would be all kinds of a fool.

He massaged the back of his neck, undecided.

Finally, he eked out a breath, opened the cabinet door, and glumly reached for a condom. This had to be his unluckiest night in his whole misbegotten life.

Meet the Author

From art student to stylist, to nurse and midwife, **Virginia Taylor**'s life has been one illogical step to the next, each one leading to the final goal of being an author. When she can tear herself away from the computer and the waiting blank page, she immerses herself in arts and crafts, gardening, or, of course, cooking. You can visit her website at www.virginia-taylor.com, and tweet her @authorvtaylor.

Printed in the United States
by Baker & Taylor Publisher Services